Alaskan Ambush

This is a work of fiction. Names, characters, businesses, places, events and incidents are either the products of the author's imagination or used in a fictitious manner. Any resemblance to actual persons, living or dead, or actual events is purely coincidental.

First Printing, 2013
ISBN-13: 978-0615827940
ISBN-10: 0615827942

Gimme Lots Publications
http://www.writerjjellis.com
brokenwifeandmom@gmail.com

For My Family
You drive me nuts sometimes but without you
I would be nothing.

Acknowledgements

My husband Tim, my editor, my 'research' assistant, my idea generator, my romance novel hero.

My Kids; Gwen, Bella, Livy, Trenton and Lily--my reason for living.

My mom Ann & my dad Charles. I'm here because of you!

My Violet Femmes, you know who you are and I appreciate the support and love you give.

My in-laws John & Alberta for giving me my first Alaskan Cruise.

My editors Gwen and Betty you don't know how much I appreciate the help.

Perkins Restaurant & Bakery in Casper, WY – you provide me with a quiet, comfortable place to work so I can get these novels done!

Alaskan Ambush

JJ Ellis

Prologue

Charlotte Mannon's Journal

January 1, 2011 - This is my first journal ever in my 60 years, do you believe that? I bought a laptop so I can just type things out instead of handwriting everything. It is supposed to be easier. Besides, I can have a password to get onto this thing so I know no one will be snooping! (And it's easy to copy and paste so all of my first entries can be the same, without risking hand cramps.)

You see, I have a top secret project that I want to organize and writing this journal is going to help me do it. I made a New Year's resolution - I am going to make sure that one by one my children get married this year. I just can't leave it up to them anymore, they just don't ever get it right. I can't believe my children don't know how to fall in love, stay in love or pick the right people.

From this point on, learning about my plan will be on a need to know basis only. I made a mistake in telling my dearest husband Ethan about my New Year's resolution, his response was: *Charlotte Mannon will you ever learn. Stay out of their lives.* Harumph! He obviously doesn't know our children very well! I'll show him! One by one our five children will get married this year, I guarantee it. Now all I have to do is find suitable partners for all of them. I have ideas, but I still need to do a bit of research and double check my facts.

I sure hope I can find Olivia's ex-boyfriend, Alex. She was so in love with him and if you ask me, they broke up for the stupidest of reasons. She doesn't think I know that reason, but I do. I'm the mom after all.

I have no idea where to begin, so I am just going to ask around and try not be too obvious about it. This should be interesting!

March 15. 2011 - I am horrible at this journal writing thing! As you can see by the amount of time that has passed since my last entry, things aren't going well. I can't find Alex anywhere! I still have a couple of leads, but I just am not sure if I can pull this off. I know how I'm going to get Mari and Graham together, but so far the plan for Olivia is a failure.

March 31, 2011 - I found Alex!!! And he is in the perfect place to enact my plan. In fact all of the kids will be set up in the same time frame. We're going to take a family cruise to Alaska, first and foremost to get Mari and Graham together, but guess where I found Alex? He is in Alaska, living in one of the ports we visit. And he runs a tourist business. Olivia is going to take a tour with her ex and they will be putty in each other's hands! You see, I figure if Alaska helped Ethan and I fall in love then it will also work its magic on the kids. I might just have to make mistakes with room arrangements, or tour arrangements or something else like that. Romance on the high seas mixed with the beauty of Alaska! What could be better?

April 11, 2011 – Things are coming along great! I am going to announce the plans for the family cruise and then all I have to do is make reservations for Olivia to go on the tour hosted by Alex. It will be on me of course, I couldn't count on her to go if she paid for it herself. If I pay, there is a built in guilt factor, and she wouldn't dare miss it. Being feared by your children can have advantages!

July 11, 2011 - Two days until D-day. Olivia and Alex aren't going to know what hit them. Reservations are made and I am even getting a bit of help from Alex's aunt and even Eleanor. This is going to be one great trip! They'll be mad at first, but someday, they will thank me. I'm sure of it.

Chapter 1

Alex Paige woke early because he had a lot of work to get done. Owning a business full time and acting as a pilot three days a week could sometimes be a daunting task, albeit not a dull one. He couldn't imagine a better way to live his life. It wasn't every day a twenty-six year old former so called slacker, owned and operated a successful floatplane tourist business with a fleet of five planes.

His two other pilots, Jason and Mark, were on duty so Alex could get caught up on the administrative tasks he considered his least favorite part of the job. But they were necessary so he wouldn't complain too much and the flying would more than make up for it. By Sunday he would be flying high.

With no time for a real breakfast, again, Alex grabbed a donut and some coffee on the way out of his cozy yellow cottage. It was a great old house in the quaint seaside community of Ketchikan, Alaska, picture perfect if a bit empty with only him living there.

Settling his tall, muscular frame into his truck, Alex turned the music up loud before pulling out onto the road. Today would be a windshield wiper kind of day, but then again what day in Ketchikan wasn't, they received almost two hundred inches of rain a year.

The office was only a few miles away and the drive there was always five minutes of solitude to help him prepare for the day ahead. This *office* was actually just a little red building near where he kept his fleet of floatplanes. If it didn't rain so much, he would forgo the building altogether and sit outside, in his true element, to work. But at least his uncle had made sure they could still see some of the beauty of the surrounding area by building a wall of picture windows along one side.

It took him a long time, but Alex finally learned that if he had to stay cooped up inside a typical office every day, he would wither away and die. He'd tried to conform, he really had, but it just hadn't worked for him. He went through twelve jobs in two years before his uncle passed away and left him the floatplane business. He'd finally found his true calling.

Of course, his favorite days were the ones when he showed tourists the beauty of Alaska. Floatplane tours over Misty Fjords National Monument or private hiking and hunting expeditions, it didn't matter. His airplane and the great outdoors were what made him happiest. In fact, he would take all of the company's tours if he could, but there was just too much business for him to handle alone now, so he had the two other pilots to help out.

As usual, his feisty white-haired assistant Pearl attacked as soon as he walked in the door. "Hey boss man, the supplier called about the update of The *Living Doll.* He needs you to call him as soon as possible."

"Okay Pearl, thanks! I'll call him now." Alex was excited about being able to finish the update to his personal plane, he couldn't wait to get back to work. At his desk, he picked up the phone and dialed the now familiar number and relief washed over him as he listened. His supplier just wanted to let him know that everything was ready and the new interior pieces would be delivered that day. Thank goodness there were no more problems. Perhaps he could start working that afternoon. It was Friday and if he started by noon, he might have the job done by Sunday. He had a big smile on his face when he hung up the phone, it looked like he would be working overtime, but it would be so worth it.

"Alex, do you want to look over the reservations for next week?" Pearl asked in the southern twang that hadn't diminished even a little bit in the twenty-five years she'd lived in Alaska.

"Sure, I guess I should see what we're up against."

He picked up the reservation sheet and since the first day on his schedule was Sunday, he started there. There was only one reservation for him in the morning and three for Mark in the afternoon. The name on his sole flight tour made his body seize up and his heart fall to the floor – *Olivia Mannon - Misty Fjords National Monument tour - reservation for four.*

It couldn't be her. She probably wouldn't leave her pampered life for all of the treasure in the world. He had to believe it wasn't her. He didn't know what he would do if he ever saw her again. "Hey Pearl, I need more details on Sunday's reservation. Where was it made from, who paid for it and how?"

"Okay kid, give me a few minutes."

Olivia had been his first love, truthfully his only true love, but things had ended badly. They just hadn't wanted the same things out of life. He'd wanted peace and nature and she'd wanted success and power. No, he didn't really think it would be her, she wouldn't be caught dead in the great outdoors, but just to be safe he would ask Jason to take the run if he didn't like the information Pearl offered him.

"Well that's strange, Alex," Pearl sounded puzzled and her brow crinkled. "The computer won't give me the usual information. All it says is Olivia Mannon reservation for four and the date. No credit card info or any contact info." She shook her head. "Very strange."

"Okay, thanks Pearl." Taking the run would be too much of a risk without additional information. He would call the software company and see if they could find out what was wrong with the reservation program, and he would ask his buddy to take his flight. As luck would have it, Jason walked in the door right then to get his tour schedule for the day.

"Hey man, I have a favor to ask," Alex queried.

"Anything boss! What is it?"

"I need you to take my run on Sunday. I'll take a run for you on Monday."

"Sure! You have a hot date or something?" Jason joked.

"Yeah right, that boy wouldn't know a hot date if it bit him on the butt," Pearl chimed in. She'd been trying to find a woman for him for the two years he'd lived there and he just wouldn't cooperate. He was stubborn and he was still madly in love with his ex-girlfriend.

Alex just ignored her comment. If he didn't love the old bat so much, she would have been out of a job the day after he'd inherited the business. Well, maybe not, after all, she was his aunt, and his uncle had requested she be well taken care of. Besides, he kind of loved her.

"Actually, Jason, I am hoping to avoid running into an old hot date," Alex informed his best friend. He was looking right at Pearl when he said it, hoping to give her a hint. All he saw was a glint in her eyes. Uh oh, that could mean big trouble.

"Okay back to work slackers!" Alex replied in his grumpiest boss voice.

Jason and Pearl just laughed and did as he said.

****

Olivia Mannon woke reeling from a dream. A dream that told her it was once again time to move on. It was actually two dreams, each a night apart, that always let her know it was time to make a change in her life. One was a nightmare that she could never remember and the other was a dream about someone she used to know.

She sat up in bed. "Jeff, get up. It's time for you to go."

"I don't have to be to work for another two hours," he mumbled from underneath a pillow.

"No, I mean it's time for you to go. For good," she stressed. "I don't think we should see each other anymore!" A little harsh, but sometimes that was how she had to do things to get her point across.

"Just like that? I thought things were good for us." He was sitting up now too.

"Yeah well, I've decided to turn over a new leaf after I get back from vacation, so bye-bye," she said as she got out of bed.

Jeff grabbed his clothes from the previous day and quickly dressed. Gathering the few other belongings he had there, he threw them into his gym bag and made his way to the door. As he walked out of the bedroom, he left Olivia with one final thought.

"You know, everyone is right about you. You are a bitch!"

Several seconds later she heard the front door slam. Sighing, she put her bathrobe on and went to join her twin brother, Jackson, in the kitchen for coffee.

"You know, he's right, you are a bitch," Jackson echoed. His head was buried in a newspaper and his right hand was wrapped around a coffee mug.

"Yeah, well at least I haven't been acting like an over emotional twit for a week like you have," she bit back.

Jackson threw his newspaper down and looked at his twin with hurt in his eyes. Standing up, he took his coffee mug to the sink and walked away from her. A few seconds later, she heard his bedroom door slam.

Great, she'd just hurt her greatest ally. Was she really that much of a bitch? Yeah, she probably was. She had been ever since…forget it, she was happy and successful, and that was all that mattered.

Olivia slumped into the nearest dining chair and dropped her head onto her arms. This day was off to a great start. Hopefully it would get better, she had a long busy day ahead.

Just as she started to think about her family's plans, the phone rang and she reluctantly got up to answer it. "Hello."

"Hi sweetie"

"Hey mom. What's up?' Olivia asked.

"I just wanted to let you know that we should be there in about forty-five minutes. Dad still has to pack the car and then it takes about twenty minutes to get to your place."

"Okay mom, we'll be ready."

"Bye darling."

"Bye mom." She hurried to wash the coffee cups and pot before heading to her bedroom to get ready. She stopped in front of Jackson's door. "Jackson?" Her hand tapped lightly on the door frame.

"Go away!" he yelled.

"I just want to let you know that mom and dad will be here in about thirty."

"Okay," he said, quieter this time.

"Jackson?" She put her hand gently on the door.

"What Olivia?" he asked.

"I'm sorry."

"I forgive you."

Olivia smiled and went to her room. This vacation was going to be fabulous, her whole family would spend an entire week being pampered onboard a luxury cruise ship as they visited Alaska. Her parents, Charlotte and Ethan, had purchased tickets for the whole family, for their annual vacation. She and Jackson would fly with their parents and the two other local Mannon children, Vanessa and Mari, to Vancouver where they would board the ship.

The last and oldest Mannon child, Abigail, would be flying in from New York City with her personal assistant Sam. Abby was the family workaholic and wasn't about to let something as trivial as an all-expenses paid family vacation get in the way of closing a big deal. Olivia missed her oldest sister a lot and couldn't wait to see her again, but having her personal assistant there would sure make for an interesting trip. How he would survive the Mannon family would be a true test of his character.

Dressed in a blue and white flowered summer dress, Olivia took one last look at herself in the mirror. She hated to admit it, but people were right about her look. Since she'd cut her long chestnut colored hair, she looked like a pixie. Her five foot four inch frame combined with her short, feminine haircut and cute features, made her look like a pixie from a children's cartoon. She really couldn't complain though, her looks had been a real asset to her over the years, and today she looked pretty good if she did say so herself. There wasn't a hair out of place and her face was fresh and glowing. Maybe she would meet someone on the cruise who would want to show her a good time. She grabbed condoms from her bathroom and put them in one of her suitcases, just in case.

She grabbed a light sweater out of the closet and headed to the living room with her bags. The sweater was for the flight, she always froze on airplanes, but she felt like wearing it right then and there. The thermostat had to be adjusted. "Hey Jackson, don't forget to turn the a/c up to eighty degrees. It doesn't need to be ten below in here while we're gone," she hollered to him as she went through the living room and kitchen making sure all lights and appliances were turned off.

"Already done," he said as he walked up behind her, suitcases in hand. He set them down next to hers and sat on the couch to wait, with that same old sad look on his face.

Everything about her tall, dark and handsome brother – his piercing green eyes, the slump of his shoulders, his walk – said that something was wrong.

"Jackson, please tell me what's going on with you. I'm really starting to get worried," she said as she sat down next to him.

"Only if you tell me why you have a new boyfriend every month when you should be married to Alex by now," he demanded, hoping the subject would get her to leave him alone. He walked to the window to look out at the street.

"Not fair Jackson." She had let Alex go three years before and no one in her wonderful family would let her forget it. Of course, she had never talked much about why she and her first love had gone their separate ways, so maybe they just needed some sort of closure. "Okay, if you won't tell me what is going on, at least tell me one thing."

"What?" he asked skeptically.

"Are you sick?" She walked over to stand near him.

He turned to her and gave her one of his famous bear hugs. "I'm fine Livia, I am perfectly healthy." He was actually smiling now.

"Okay, I believe you. Now, let's go wait outside for mom and dad. The sooner we get this vacation started, the better we'll both feel!" And the sooner she got the vacation started, the sooner she would stop thinking about Alex. Damn her brother for bringing him up!

****

Jackson put their carry-on bags in the overhead compartment and took his seat next to the window. Olivia sat in the middle seat right next to him and there was no one in the aisle seat, which made her happy. She would have her brother all to herself for *The Inquisition.* "So, if I tell you more about why Alex and I broke up, will you really tell me what's wrong with you?" she asked once they were leveling off.

"I can't yet. I have a lot to think about before I tell anyone," he stressed. "Please be patient, you'll know soon enough." He never thought Olivia would contemplate going through with talking about her ex, her lips were usually sealed when it came to Alex Paige.

"You can't even tell your twin huh?" she questioned. "It must be something big."

Jackson just nodded and turned to look sadly out the window. 'How about you tell me about your break up with Alex now and I'll tell you my news before I tell the rest of the family," he offered.

"I don't know Jackson, is that fair?"

"Just an idea," he mumbled, still looking out the window.

Olivia felt so bad for her brother, his heart was so heavy right now. Okay, she could do this, she could open up to him. After all, they were twins, as close as could be. She decided to tell him what he'd wanted to know for three long years. "Alex and I broke up because of his lack of ambition. It just didn't mesh well with the kind of life I wanted." Olivia took a deep, steadying breath. It always sounded so awful when she heard it out loud. "Did you know, he had twelve jobs in two years? His grandfather even offered to lend him money to buy a business in Henderson, but nothing ever seemed to satisfy him," she confided.

"We all know more than you think, Livia."

"You do?"

He chuckled. "Yeah, I just wanted to hear your say it out loud so you could realize how ridiculous it sounds."

"You jerk!"

"Did you love him?" Jackson looked pointedly at her.

"Yes. Very much," she answered quietly. "I wanted to marry him."

"Then why did the rest matter, Olivia?" he asked pained.

Olivia sighed heavily. This was the exact response she expected. No one ever understood. "It just did. He was camp outdoors, I was presidential suite at a five star hotel." She leaned her head back against the seat, thinking about her old love. "You don't understand do you? You know, that's why I didn't talk about it much."

Jackson looked at his sister with something close to anger in his eyes.

But Olivia spoke before he could. "I know, I'm a bitch right?"

Jackson just smirked and started to read the airline magazine.

Olivia had her answer. Her best friend and twin truly did think she was a bitch. And in all actuality, she was, but she couldn't change that now. She put headphones on and closed her eyes. Thoughts of Alex, and the first time they met flooded her mind.

She was nineteen years old and just days away from final exams for her sophomore year in college. It was so hot outside, the first hundred and ten degree day of the year, and it had come early. Olivia's hands were full of books, she was sweaty, and her long straight hair was plastered to her face when a tall, black haired, brown eyed guy walked up beside her and relieved her of some of her burden.

"Let me help you," was all he said. A lock of his tousled black hair fell over his left eye and her heart skipped a beat or two. He

was tall and defined, he made her feel so small. And when he looked at her, his deep brown eyes saw everything, it was like they could read her every thought. She wasn't the least bit scared of him, despite his size and piercing gaze, he was somehow comfortable to be around. And he was such a life saver.

She was too hot to even ask his name, the less energy she used, the more likely she was to survive the heat. Especially since she had to drive twenty-five miles with a broken air conditioner.

Walking along in comfortable silence, they quickly reached her car and he handed the books back to her. He jogged away without a word, and Olivia didn't even have a chance to ask his name or to say thank you.

That weekend, once finals were over and she was an official junior in the College of Hotel Administration, there was a big party at one of her friends' houses. It was an annual bash to celebrate the end of yet another school year, and this would be Olivia's second one. They were usually really fun, but for some reason she wasn't sure she was up to it this time. She came very close to staying home, but her best friend, Chloe, finally talked her into going. She decided she would give it one hour and then she would head home.

Forty-five minutes later, Olivia was sitting there nursing a beer and wishing it was time to leave when she saw him – the handsome stranger who had helped her carry her books on that scorching day. Chickening out twice, she was finally able to approach him to thank him for his help and they ended up talking through the night.

Everything about him excited her, especially that stray lock of hair that kept falling over his eye, and she could hardly wait to get to know him better. Right away she found out that he was a Liberal Arts major from Seattle, he was twenty-one years old, and his name was Alexander Timothy Paige Jr. The rest she would learn over the next few months, and have one hell of a time doing it.

They had their first date the next day, and were together every day after that – they were inseparable. She went with him on his vacation to the coast of Oregon late that summer where they spent their days on the beach and their nights alone in his parent's summer cottage, making love.

When summer ended, Olivia was so incredibly sad to have to go back to school, to work, and to the suffocating heat that she cried for over an hour. He held her and kissed her until she quieted, and then he rushed into town, coming back with a single pink rose and a promise that anytime she was unhappy or hurt he would bring her one. He never broke that promise, not even once. A single pink rose had been delivered to her apartment the day after she broke up with him.

Olivia had been determined to live a life where she never wanted for anything, and Alex couldn't help her achieve that life. He was never happy with his jobs and never tried to get more than an entry level position. So she ended it. No matter how much she loved him. No matter how much she grieved for the loss of the only person she had ever truly loved.

****

Alex was thrilled! He'd just finished the makeover of his personal plane, The *Living Doll,* well ahead of schedule. It took him four hours, that's it, it wasn't even dinner time yet. He couldn't wait to take her up in the air again and his next run would be Monday since he'd traded shifts with Jason. She was his personal plane, but he used her for tour flights too, how could he not share the joy of The *Living Doll* with everyone! Hell, he wouldn't wait until Monday, he had to take her up immediately. He did all of his preflight checks and before he knew it he was soaring again. What a rush it was to feel so free. Up here he had no worries, he could be who he wanted to be.

As he flew his usual route through Misty Fjord he couldn't help but wonder what Olivia would think of it, if in fact she saw it on Sunday. She was such a classy girl, she would probably ooh and ah but not see the real beauty. When they'd visited Seattle one time he thought for sure the beautiful scenery they'd hiked through had finally broken through her uptight personality, but alas, it hadn't. She was the same old Olivia when they arrived home. Seattle didn't hold all bad memories for him though. He'd never forget one trip he took to Seattle.

He and Olivia had known each other for twenty-one fantastic days when he had to go to Seattle to visit his parents for a week. They had decided that the night before he left would be their first time together. They were both excited and nervous, but ready to take their relationship to the next step.

Olivia had wanted to take him out to dinner because she was a horrible cook, even though she was a management intern at a multi star restaurant, but Alex had come up with a completely different plan. He'd decided to cook her a gourmet meal. His intent had been to charm her and make her feel comfortable. He'd even set the mood with candlelight, wine and romantic music.

By the time she'd taken her last delicate bite, he'd wanted her so badly he couldn't stand it. He started to clean up after dinner because he didn't want to seem like he was rushing things, but she started to kiss him while he was standing at the sink, and when she whispered to him exactly what she wanted to do to him, he came completely unglued. They made it as far as the bathroom where they stopped to grab condoms. They had sex for the first time standing against the bathroom wall. It was the most thrilling thing either of them had ever experienced. No one else had ever made him lose his senses like that and Olivia had claimed the same. Later that night, after things had calmed down and they were laying entwined together in bed, the words I love you *were uttered for the first time.*

Alex didn't usually let himself indulge in that memory, it was one of the few that was usually off limits. This time though, he couldn't help it. It made him ache with missing her but it was still too dangerous to chance seeing her, if in fact she was going to be in town on Sunday. He would lock himself in his house and not come out until all of the ships left the dock. And then he would call Jason and ask him to describe the mystery passenger and her guests. How could he not?

Chapter 2

Olivia was shaking and breathing hard. The dreams, again, only this time, both in the same night. No matter how hard she tried she couldn't remember the dream that scared the daylights out of her. She just knew she was scared. She heard screaming and something that could have been swishing or splashing. It never really settled in enough to take on a true shape or meaning.

The second dream on the other hand had the potential to leave her even more breathless.

She started out walking down the main walkway at the University, headed past the performing arts center, the library, the alumni center, and the humanities building, but it was like she was on one of those airport moving walkways. She assumed she was headed to the Student Union to look for Alex but she couldn't be sure about what her destination was, because the walkway was always switching directions. It would stop moving long enough for her to catch a glimpse of Alex and when she would venture toward him and call his name he would disappear.

She would follow him into every building on the way back to her car, where she'd begun her journey. The desperation to find him nearly blinded her. She would see a friend and ask if they'd seen him and they would say yes and tell her where he was and she would go searching for him there. Eventually she ended up back at her car and Alex would be sitting in the passenger seat. "I found you," *she would say while smiling at him. He would lean toward her and just as their lips touched, he would disappear.*

She was left with fear, anxiety, desire and if she really got down to it, a bit of sadness. She was always left rattled to the core. This time was even worse, because she wasn't supposed to have both dreams in one night. A night apart is how it had always been. And then she would make a big change in her life. But she'd already done that. Jeff was gone, she'd interviewed for a promotion and she'd thought seriously about buying a bigger home. There was absolutely nothing else to change, but she had a nagging feeling on that cloudy, cool morning in the Inside Passage of Alaska, that there was.

"Vanessa! Get up." She called as she hopped down off the Pullman bed and headed to the bathroom. "I want breakfast."

"I'm trying to sleep." Vanessa mumbled back, but climbed out of bed anyway. "Hurry up in there, I need to pee, I'm going to the gym before breakfast so you're on your own."

Olivia hurried through her shower and walked out of the bathroom wrapped in a towel. "Why the gym so early Nessa?"

"I need to burn off some frustration before I face the rest of the human race," she smirked.

"Ooh, is sexy Thomas getting to you?" Olivia was hopeful. Jackson's best friend Thomas had been invited on the cruise to help him relax after coming home from Afghanistan with a hip injury. He was one sexy Marine and he had a stormy past with Vanessa.

"Humph, hardly! He's an annoying ass, just like he was in school," but her face was turning redder than her hair.

"Okay, so he's an annoying, very sexy ass," Olivia teased.

Vanessa hurried into the bathroom and locked the door. She heard Olivia laughing at her as she started the shower.

****

Alex woke to a loud knocking on his front door. He didn't have to go to work so he'd stayed up until two a.m. researching ways to spruce up the business. He'd planned to sleep until at least ten. It was seven thirty. Who the hell was knocking before nine a.m.? When he stumbled to the door and pulled it open Pearl was standing there with a box in her arms and two on the ground beside her.

"You sick? You're never in bed this late," she barked as she pushed her way inside. "Grab the other two boxes for me will ya!"

Alex stepped outside, grabbed the boxes and took them to the coffee table where Pearl had taken hers.

"Well boy, are ya sick?" she asked again.

"No, I just stayed up late is all."

"Thinkin' about the ex were ya?" she teased.

"No, actually I wasn't, but now I am. Thanks Auntie." He dodged a smack to his arm.

"I'm sorry about that Alex, but that doesn't mean you can call me auntie."

He laughed. "What's in the boxes?"

"Found em in the garage when I was trying to find that old 70th birthday banner for

Millie's party next week." She told him. "These boxes are yours and were stuck up in the rafters."

"Didn't realize I was missing anything," he stated. "Guess I'll have to give them a peek later."

"Well, back to my day! See ya later kid." That quickly, Pearl was gone and the front door slammed behind her.

Alex was left sitting there looking at the boxes, wondering what the hell was inside.

He made some coffee and grabbed a muffin before sitting down on the couch and pulling the lid off of the first box. It was filled with old papers, some from high school, and some from college. Most of it was just crap that he didn't need anymore. He kept a trash bag by his side and threw away paper after paper that he had no idea why he'd kept.

The second box held an old martial arts uniform from when he was in Jr. High School and a bunch of other Jr. High mementos. Those would be re boxed and put into his own garage.

The third box was a jumble of many different things, of more recent memories. On second glance, they were all memories involving Olivia; ticket stubs from their first movie, a program from a symphony at the University, a stuffed animal she had given him, restaurant receipts, a t-shirt with an obscene slogan that she got him for his birthday, a picture of them together at his college graduation, a crystal teddy bear she'd given him for an anniversary, the packet of information he'd requested on how to become a park ranger because he thought he'd finally found a job he could love and succeed at, and the ring he'd been planning to give to her.

Before he could propose, she'd called the relationship off, and his parents' vacation home in Oregon had become his escape for a year before he moved to Alaska to help Pearl in her time of need, and to accept his inheritance.

He quickly closed the box and taped it shut so it could be moved to the garage as soon as possible. He left out only the crystal teddy bear, the picture and the ring.

The delicate crystal statue was carried over to the entertainment center and put front and center on an empty shelf. "I miss you, Olivia," he whispered before walking back to the couch. He still missed her so much, but he could not chance seeing her again, he couldn't risk the pain. Could he?

He sat for a while staring at the picture of them together. The desert sun glinted off of her dark hair. She looked like an angel. Her green eyes were sparkling with happiness and her smile was big and bright. She was absolutely stunning. Alex remembered what had happened next like it was only moments before. She'd turned to him with love shining in her eyes. "I'm so proud of you!" she'd said. Too bad she hadn't always been. Toward the end of their relationship there had been more disappointment than anything.

Alex set the picture aside, opened the ring box, and smiled. It was a beautiful old ring. His grandmother had given it to him when he told her he wanted to marry Olivia. Grandma Lily had recently been diagnosed with terminal cancer and knew she didn't have long to live so she took both rings off of her finger then and there and put them in his palm, wrapping his fingers tightly around them. "I love Olivia and I want her to have these," she'd said. "Your grandfather and I both do. You two remind me of him and I when we were young."

When Olivia broke things off, he vowed never to use the rings, he would pass them down to his kids instead, if he ever had any.

He took the picture and the little jeweler's box and put them in his night stand drawer before fixing a quick lunch and heading to The *Living Doll.* He needed to fly.

****

Olivia and Jackson walked out of their rooms at the same time.

"Want some company for breakfast?" He asked.

"Absolutely!" Olivia answered. "Dining Room or Café Wave?"

"Café, we won't have to share a table with strangers."

They walked quietly together to the café and filled their plates before taking a seat near the windows that looked out over the calming waters.

"What do you have planned for today?" Jackson asked between bites.

"I have no clue," Olivia answered. "I think I'm going to have an idle day, which of course I hate."

"You don't have to be idle, there's so much to do onboard sis."

She sighed and sank down in her seat. "I know, I just feel so, I don't know, restless I guess. You should entertain me!" she hinted. "Are you ready to talk yet?"

Jackson quirked his eyebrow at his twin. "I don't know, are you ready to start feeling guilty for what you did to Alex?" he questioned.

Olivia gasped, she was truly shocked. "How dare you Jack? I feel guilty all the damn time, but there is nothing I can do about it now."

"Livia, I didn't mean..."

"No Jackson don't. Do you know what is in that little lockbox under my bed?" she asked.

"No, but I'm sure you'll tell me."

"Twenty seven apology letters to Alex," she confessed.

"That's a start." Jackson admitted. "Maybe you should have sent one."

Olivia threw her napkin on top of her plate and fled the dining room with tears in her eyes. Jackson was so right, she should have sent one of the letters a long time ago. Not that she would have wanted to go back to him, but she really should have apologized for being such a selfish bitch. She couldn't help it, she was who she was and there was no changing that.

Olivia walked around the ship not knowing what to do with herself. The guilt threatened to eat her alive right on the spot. She walked through the shops but only made it halfway before getting bored. Next she tried miniature golf but stopped when her lack of concentration almost got a little boy smacked upside the head with a ball. One thing that did give her a bit of peace of mind was swimming in the adult's only pool. She concentrated on the caress of the water and keeping her breathing even instead of on her past mistakes.

After the swim she felt almost human again and decided to track Vanessa down and con her into going to lunch. When her sister was nowhere to be found, Olivia ended up seeking out her parents. They were more than happy to have lunch with her and she got the feeling that her idea could be a huge mistake.

"Are you having fun dear?" Charlotte asked as they sat down in a booth in the café wave.

"Kind of," she started. "So much to do here that I just can't decide I guess." A little fib wouldn't hurt. She didn't want her parents to feel bad because she wasn't allowing herself to have a good time.

"Are you sure everything is okay sweetie?" Ethan asked, patting her hand.

"Jackson says she's been mopey because of Alex," Charlotte interjected.

Olivia dropped her fork but recovered quickly. "I have not been mopey over Alex," she ground out. "If you people would stop bringing him up, I might not think about him at all!" She was blind with rage and the only thing that kept her from going off on her mother was the consistent pressure of her dad's hand on her arm.

"I'm sorry if I offended you dear," was all Charlotte said.

"It's okay mother," Olivia sighed. "Just please don't' bring *his* name up again."

"Of course not, Livia," Ethan answered for the both of them.

****

Alex did his pre-flight checks and headed The *Living Doll* toward Juneau. He didn't have his uncle Peter or his father to talk to so he would talk to his friends John and Sue.

The whole flight he couldn't stop thinking of his relationship with Olivia; when they met, the first date, the first time they made love, their first vacation together, the first time he took her up in an airplane, and of course their breakup. In the over two hour flight he went through every emotion he knew of, and by the time he reached John and Sue's cabin he felt like he'd been through a wringer, twice.

As was usual with his friends, the minute he knocked he was ushered in and made to feel at home.

"You don't look so good son!" John exclaimed when he brought Alex a cup of coffee.

"I'm not doing so good, John." He smiled and took a sip of the strong, warm brew. "I've had some old memories brought up recently and they are *killing* me."

"What kind of old memories, Alex?" Sue asked, walking in from the kitchen.

Alex proceeded to tell them about the possible visit from the only woman he'd ever loved. The woman he still loved. They already knew the history behind the relationship so his story was short.

"I don't know what to do. In one way, I would kill to see her and in another I can't bear the thought of setting eyes on her again," Alex bemoaned. "If I see her it will end the same way. She won't have changed."

"How can you be so sure, Alex?" Sue questioned. "You've changed, maybe she has too."

Alex shrugged, "Maybe." He ran his hands through his hair. "What would you do?"

"Well," John stated. "I myself would want to see her. Not take her tour, but I would find a way to see her."

"Yep," Sue agreed. "You need some closure."

"You're probably right." Alex sighed. "I need to see her no matter how much it hurts." He could hang around the docks or near the plane. He would have to wear a hat and sunglasses so she wouldn't recognize him if she happened to see him. Come the next day, he would be transforming himself into the ultimate stalker.

"Okay, now that, that is settled, are you staying the night?" Sue asked.

"Nah, but I sure could use one of your fabulous home cooked dinners," Alex replied.

"Dinner it is!" Sue enthused. She loved how Alex appreciated her cooking even though he was the gourmet.

With a full, happy stomach, Alex climbed back in The *Living Doll* and flew home. He was on his couch watching TV by eight p.m.

Chapter 3

Olivia woke on the third day of the cruise and looked around her cabin. Her sister Marjorie was still asleep with a smile on her face, probably dreaming about her soon to be ex, and her sister Vanessa was snoring in the bed below her.

She was excited to start the morning. Day two had been less than exciting, walking around the ship, swimming, mini golf and shopping with her sisters had been okay, just a bit boring for her expectations of a great vacation. This day would be fun though, she would get to go flying over Misty Fjord National Monument and explore a new town. Today she would not be idle in the least.

“Vanessa, wake up,” she hissed as she tossed a pillow at her sister’s head.

“What do you want?” Vanessa moaned quietly.

"I want you to come to town with me before the tour later," she whispered as she climbed down gracefully off of the Pullman bed. "Or are you too tired from hanging out with Tommy boy last night?

Vanessa smirked. "God! Can't I just sleep in one day on this cruise?" In response to the remark about Thomas, she took her sister's pillow and threw it, hitting her in the head.

Olivia laughed. "Nope, too much fun to be had to waste time on sleeping!"

Mari stirred in her bed and Olivia reminded herself to be quiet. Her older sister didn't need to wake up yet.

"Okay just let me get ready." Vanessa sighed. "I'm first in the shower though."

Olivia rushed into the bathroom and locked the door behind her. She heard something hit the door and laughed out loud.

"Since when are you in a good mood? You've been moping around for two days thinking about Alex," Vanessa hollered to her sister.

Mari moaned and sat up. "Shut up you two!" Then she lay back down and covered her head with her pillow.

Olivia shrugged even though no one could see her. She *had* been moping around about Alex because her twin wouldn't stop bringing him up. But she'd met a nice guy in one of the bars the night before and had decided it was time to concentrate on something other than the past, a past that could not be changed.

As she stepped under the warm shower spray she couldn't help but think about what her sisters would be going through on this trip. Her mother was setting them up. Mari with her soon to be ex-husband of convenience who had magically appeared on the ship with his daughter and mother in tow, Vanessa and their childhood friend Thomas, and Abigail and her personal assistant Sam. Being set up must really suck. She was grateful that her mom hadn't been able to find someone to push on her. She would be free to enjoy herself and do whatever she wanted to, and just thinking about *that* made her relax.

She couldn't wait to get into Ketchikan and do a bit of shopping before she flew off into the wild with her sister, her twin and Thomas. She loved to fly in small planes and she couldn't wait to experience that indescribable feeling again.

Vanessa tapping on the door broke into her reverie. "Hurry up, Livia," she whispered loudly.

Olivia sighed and turned the water off. She'd better get out before Vanessa broke the door down.

****

It was seven a.m. on his day off when the phone rang, waking Alex from a deep sleep. Dreams had troubled him until about four o'clock, after that, he had finally slept well.

"Hello," he answered sleepily

"Alex, its Pearl"

"Why are you calling so early, is everything okay?"

"Everything is fine Alex, I'm calling to let you know that Jason can't take the eleven o'clock today. His wife's flight from Orlando was cancelled because of severe thunderstorms and his babysitter is sick so he has to stay with the kiddos until the missus gets home."

"Okay Pearl, thanks for letting me know." Alex hung up the phone and got out of bed. If he was going to work after all, he really should shower and shave. Yes, he had showered the previous night, but he woke up covered in sweat more than once because of dreams of Olivia. And then suddenly he remembered, the eleven o'clock flight that he was going to do for Jason was the Olivia Mannon flight. Where the hell was his brain? He didn't want to admit that it had been in his pants for the last forty-eight hours, along with thoughts of loving *her*. He absolutely had to find someone to cover for him - after the shower.

The hot water beating on his tight muscles did nothing to relax Alex. He couldn't get Olivia out of his head. He wondered what she was doing right that second. Was she at home in Henderson eating breakfast? Was she on a cruise ship just pulling into Ketchikan? His body started to react to thoughts of her eating at his favorite restaurant, walking down the same boardwalk on Creek Street that he loved to walk down himself, walking through his living room in her bare feet, slipping into the shower with him. *She didn't really like shower sex, but she used to love to slip in and have him wash her hair. As soon as it was rinsed she would turn to him, her hand traveling down his abdomen to take him into her hand. Her caresses and strokes drove him mad. She always brought him to the brink before slipping out of the shower. She would wait on the bed for him, completely ready. He would crawl up to her and drive himself inside. She completely enveloped him, so tight and slick. Her whimpers and sighs mingling with his moans. They became one as they moved together, giving and taking until they both threw caution to the wind and came together in crashing waves.*

"Oh God!" Alex moaned, collapsing against the side of the shower stall. His body finally relaxed, but his mind still raced with fear, regret and heartache. "It's been three years, how can you still have this effect on me, Olivia?"

Rinsing one last time, he turned the water off and stepped out of the shower not even bothering to dry off. He just wrapped the towel around his lean waist and walked dripping to the phone in his bedroom, to dial Pearls number.

Damn he was cold. Taking the towel from his waist, he started to dry himself off. As he was running it through his hair, Pearl finally answered.

"Howdy"

"Hey Pearl. I need you to call Mark and have him take that eleven o'clock for me," Alex said desperately.

"I wondered when you would remember it was Olivia's flight," she laughed. "I already called Mark. His son's birthday is today and he can't be there until the afternoon shift."

"Damn Pearl, you've got to help me out here. Can't you baby-sit Jason's kids for him or something?" he asked

"No can do kiddo. I have commitments! I guess you will just have to take a deep breath and take it yourself. What's the worst that could happen? She doesn't bite does she?"

"She does more than bite, Pearl. That's what I'm afraid of." He sighed loudly as he threw the towel across the room. What in the hell would he do now?

"Hey Alex," Pearl said tentatively

"What?" he asked grumpily.

"I hope this *is* the Olivia."

"Why?" he asked surprised. His groin reacted again to the image of Olivia walking along the boardwalk, his boardwalk, in his town.

"You've been pining for her all this time. You need to set things straight and get on with your life...with or without her."

Alex didn't want to hear that, especially now when she might be arriving in town any minute. "Pearl, if it is her, I'm doomed."

He quickly hung up the phone and went to shave. The flight would take a lot of mental preparation. He was going to be a nervous wreck and he couldn't let it affect his flying. Why him? Why now?

By the time Alex was dressed and on his way to the office, he had convinced himself that this passenger was not going to be sexy, beautiful Olivia Mannon from Nevada. He put pictures of a sweet old grandma named Olivia into his mind and urged them to stay there all morning.

****

"Come on Nessa! I want to get into town to explore and back here to leave our packages before the flight." Olivia was exasperated with her baby sister, she was always so slow at getting ready.

"I'm coming, Livia!" Vanessa called from the bathroom. "I want to look my best."

"Yeah, for Tommy boy," Olivia teased. "Bet you're glad mom bought him a ticket huh?"

Vanessa was blushing ten shades of red when she came out of the bathroom. "Let's just go!" she snipped.

Olivia made up for the teasing by giving her sister a hug. They heard "Finally, some quiet!" as they walked out the door. They giggled all the way to the elevator.

Stepping onto the gangplank at the same time, they took a good look around. "Kinda small," Vanessa remarked as she took in the view of Ketchikan. She was a city girl through and through.

Olivia was too, or so she thought. The quaint little town took her breath away. She actually felt quite comfortable there. "Most places in Alaska are small Nessa," Olivia laughed. "I kind of like it."

Vanessa looked at her sister and raised her hand to feel her forehead for a fever.

Olivia smacked her away. "Stop it. I'm not sick you big dork. I actually like this place."

Vanessa mumbled her way down the gangplank and Olivia just followed, chuckling to herself.

Olivia had originally wanted to shop, but now she just wanted to walk around and explore, but of course Vanessa wanted to shop and get back to the ship. They bickered for almost a block when they finally came to a compromise. They would quickly explore Ketchikan's famous former red-light district and then head to the shops.

Olivia took the town map that she'd picked up from the visitor's center on the dock and plotted their course. "Hey Vanessa, that green building over there is a former house of ill repute." Her baby sister had a weird obsession with the history of the world's oldest profession. She'd even done a term paper on the history of prostitution in Nevada her senior year in college.

"Okay, so maybe this town isn't so bad," Vanessa admitted as she pulled Olivia toward the little green building. As the youngest Mannon child took her time exploring the museum that was now housed in the former whore house, Olivia stepped outside and looked out over Ketchikan Creek, which wound and roared below the boardwalk.

The sound of the creek was something she could never get tired of. For the first time in a long time, maybe for the first time since she was a child, she felt at peace with herself. Even thoughts of Alex, brought on by his love of old boardwalks, didn't rile her up.

"Hey sis," Vanessa stated, coming up behind her. "You ready to find a place to have breakfast? I'm starving!"

Olivia smiled. "Yeah, let's go." They headed back toward the commercial district and stopped at a quaint little café with a for sale sign in the window. Olivia dreamed of owning her own restaurant, not a little hometown joint like this, but an upscale place with stars in the rating system. Someone would be lucky to get this place though, it was cute and eclectic. Each round table had a different colored gingham tablecloth and each stool at the counter had a different colored gingham seat. Olivia had never felt so enraptured by an eating establishment. She spent most of her time catering to the rich and famous in a black tie only restaurant that the average person could never afford.

Each color coded table had a menu holder with four matching menus in it. Olivia and Vanessa picked the 'orange' table and sat down to make their selections. They both ordered Denver Omelets and coffee from the friendly waitress and started to map out a strategy for their shopping adventure. It was obvious that Vanessa had everything already planned out so Olivia let her go at it while she stared out the window, thinking about the day ahead. She couldn't wait to get up in the air. Floatplanes were so much fun, Alex had taken her up in his dad's many times when they were dating. She absolutely loved it.

"Does that sound like a good plan?" Vanessa asked. "Olivia…sweetie, what's wrong?" Vanessa shook her sister's arm.

Olivia let out an almost mournful squeak. "Alex." She whispered.

"Alex?" Vanessa asked. "Where?"

"Yeah," Olivia returned. "I swear I saw him go into that shop across the street." She was slightly trembling and pale.

"Couldn't have been sis," Vanessa answered.

"I've got to go find out!" Olivia exclaimed as she stood to leave.

"Not leaving already are ya?" the waitress asked as she set their plates on the table in front of them. "The food is really good and you look a bit shaky. Sit and eat sweetie, don't want someone passing out on my watch."

"Um, yeah, thanks," Olivia mumbled as she sat back down to try to eat. There is no way that could have been Alex anyway, her mind was just playing tricks on her because Jackson couldn't keep his big mouth shut.

"Can I get you anything else?" the waitress asked, still looking at Olivia with concern in her eyes.

"Uh, no, no thanks Millie," Vanessa said, looking at the waitress's name tag.

"Oh, I'm not Millie, I'm just filling in for her for the breakfast and lunch shifts. The name is Pearl." She smiled at the two young women.

The name Pearl rang a distant bell but Olivia couldn't quite pinpoint it. "Well thank you Pearl, I think we're good for now."

"Alrighty then, just holler if ya need anything," she exclaimed as she walked away to help other customers.

Olivia noticed that through the whole meal, the waitress kept a close eye on her. Not only was Ketchikan a beautiful town, but the people were super friendly too, she almost didn't want to leave this place...almost, but not quite.

****

Alex's cell phone rang and he picked it up on the third ring. "Paige Air Tours, this is Alex. How can I help you?" Pearl had her other 'commitments' so he'd forwarded the business phone to his cell.

"Hey Alex, it's Pearl. I'm fillin' in for Millie at The Dock Stop. Come on over and have some breakfast before your flight."

"I can barely hear your Pearl, why so quiet for once in your life," he teased.

"Don't want to disturb the customers, smart ass," she retorted "You coming or not?"

"Can't, I've got a lot to do this morning. After I pick up these key chain gifts for my passengers, I'm going to the docks to give The *Doll* a good polish."

"Okay kid, just promise me you'll eat something before you fly." Pearl said concerned.

"I have something in the truck. I'll eat before I go up," he promised.

"You better!" and she hung up.

Alex laughed and put his phone back in his pocket. His aunt was worse than his mother had ever been.

"Hey Jessie, I'm outta here," Alex called to the back room of the souvenir shop where he bought tiny seaplane key chains with the Paige Air Tours logo on it. "Pearl will have a check to you first of the month as usual."

"See ya next time, Alex!" Jessie called back. "Fly safe as always."

Walking out the door and over to his truck, he decided to sit there and eat before he headed to the docks. A giant muffin and a thermos of black coffee wasn't much but it would hold him until lunch. His stomach was still nervous about meeting the little old lady, or so he hoped, named Olivia Mannon.

Halfway through his meal, he leaned his head against the seat rest and took a few deep breaths to focus himself. Fate would not be so cruel as to bring him face to face with the one person he couldn't stop loving but could never have. Would it?

He sat up startled and bumped his head on the roof of the truck. "I said wait up sis, my legs are a lot shorter than yours!" came from behind him. Shit, it couldn't be! He threw the truck door open and jumped out. He ran to the back and looked in all directions. All he saw were three cars driving by on the street and a short haired woman quickly disappearing around the corner.

He really must be hallucinating. Hearing Olivia's voice when she was nowhere to be seen was just crazy. Either that or the short haired woman sounded a hell of a lot like Olivia. At least he could rest assured that she wasn't Olivia. His ex would never have cut her long locks and she always had blonde highlights where this stranger's hair was only brown. The scariest part was, after three years, he still remembered the sweetness of her voice.

****

Olivia stood next to the giant rain gauge on the dock waiting for Vanessa, Thomas and Jackson to join her for the walk to the float plane base. After breakfast they'd done some shopping and stored their packages back on the ship. She'd been so excited to get up in the air that she left the others behind to find their own way. The ship seemed somehow suffocating when the fresh air and beauty of Ketchikan was waiting. It didn't escape her that it was kind of ironic that she was feeling that way. She normally *hated* fresh air and wilderness, but for some reason, on this particular day, she was giddy with excitement to be outside in these beautiful surroundings. She had a habit of always being on time or early, whereas Vanessa was always late, had she waited for her siblings and friend, she would have been way too restless

Olivia looked away from the gauge and back at the ship when Vanessa and Thomas came walking down the gangplank hand in hand. That was a complete shocker. Olivia just kind of stared at their intertwined hands. They had been like oil and water as kids, except for a brief time when they'd been more like the perfect oil and vinegar mixture - tangy and working well in unison.

Olivia decided not to embarrass the cute new couple…yet. "Hey, where is Jackson?" She asked when she realized her twin was nowhere in sight.

"He's not coming," Thomas exclaimed. "Said something about finding a library and a cheap internet connection."

"Whatever that means," Vanessa added.

Now Olivia was even more curious about what was going on with her brother. Why spend a glorious vacation researching something on the internet? But that was his loss and she wouldn't worry about it until she had a chance to talk to him. "Okay, let's go then! We don't want to be late."

Olivia followed the directions her mother had given her and before long, they were close enough to hear tour boats and seaplanes starting to come to life.

"Livia!" Vanessa called out. "We'll catch up."

When Olivia turned, she saw Vanessa holding both of Thomas' hands. He was obviously in some kind of distress. Thomas was said to have moments where his time in the war came rushing back to him and too many voices intruding made things worse. It was best if she stayed out of it and let Vanessa deal with it.

She walked away, toward the sign that announced *FLOAT PLANE TOURS HERE.* About an eighth of a mile down the dock she saw a large ramp leading down to three or four floatplane slips. Olivia didn't know which company her flight was with so she finally broke out the information her mother had put in her travel folder, it was in the very back so she had to dig for it. A little blue piece of note paper that she'd found folded into a small square at the bottom of the folder, said their flight was hosted by Paige Air Tours.

Olivia felt all of the blood rush out of her head. Alex's uncle owned a business with that same name, only it was based in Washington or Oregon. Wasn't it? That's where his *whole* family was from. Wasn't it?

What the hell. Could she ever escape memories of that man? If it wasn't one thing, it was another and if this was his uncle, she hoped he wouldn't recognize her. She'd only met him, briefly, once in Vegas when he was there visiting. She didn't really feel like getting involved with her ex's life, even if it was only for a brief period of time. She sighed heavily and kept her feet moving. Now, for some reason, she wasn't looking forward to her flight tour anymore.

The pilot had his back to Olivia as she approached the Paige Air Tours slip. She knew immediately that Alex's uncle wasn't the pilot. She would have recognized the actual pilot's jean clad ass anywhere.

"Ah fuck!" slipped out of her mouth before she could even think.

"Well hello to you too, Living Doll." Alex turned. She couldn't see his heart beating out of control under his flannel shirt, and for that he was forever grateful.

Chapter 4

It seemed that his eleven o'clock passenger was indeed *the* Olivia Mannon. Only she had cut her long, beautiful hair. It was short, sassy and all one color. He really liked it. Was it possible that she was even more beautiful than the last time he'd seen her?

"Hello Alex, how are you?" Olivia inquired sounding much calmer than she felt. Inside she was falling apart.

"Good! And you?"

"Good!" Her heart was beating way too fast and she had an annoying heat spreading through her body, but other than that she was fine, really. She felt like she wanted to run away as fast as she could but Vanessa and Thomas walked up behind her, blocking her halfhearted plan of escape.

"Alex, you remember Vanessa and Thomas."

"Hi Vanessa," Alex nodded at her. "All grown up and even more beautiful."

"Thank you Alex!" She smiled. "Three years changes a lot."

"Thomas," he said as the two men shook hands. "It's been a really long time man. Really missing those late night poker games."

"Same here," Thomas stated. "We lost everyone; you left, I went active military, Graham couldn't stand being too near Mari and Jackson was always busy so the old group disbanded."

"Sorry to hear that." Alex said. "We had some great times."

"Yes, we did," Thomas returned.

Alex reached out and touched Olivia's arm. "Well, if we're going to leave on time I'd better finish up my preflight checks, so if you'll excuse me," and he walked away.

Olivia turned to Vanessa and instinctively grabbed her sister for comfort. Vanessa wrapped her arms around her and squeezed tight.

"What am I going to do?" Olivia cried, quietly. What would the next few hours be like? Should she pretend like nothing was wrong, should she just treat him like an old friend? God, why had this happened?

"It's okay sis!" Vanessa reassured her. "Just relax and have fun."

Her sister was right, she just had to act natural. It was the only way she would survive the day. Then she had the stray thought that if she did what came naturally with Alex, she would have to throw him down and do what she desired most. Right that minute it meant she would kiss him and never let him go. She quickly pushed that little thought aside.

"Will your number four be here soon?" Alex inquired as he walked back over to them.

"He's not coming." Olivia said sadly, wishing Jackson was there with her. "My twin deserted us."

Alex breathed a huge, silent sigh of relief that she hadn't been looking sad over a boyfriend or a husband standing her up.

"Well then, should we get this show on the road?" Alex asked his three passengers.

"Let's go!" they all said in unison.

He helped Vanessa and Thomas onto the plane and then the three other passengers who were also waiting, but he shut the door before Olivia could climb in. He motioned for her to sit next to him in the front and she didn't argue.

For Olivia, it felt good to be so close to him again, at least for the most part. She just wouldn't let herself think about what would happen when the tour was over.

****

Alex's reaction to seeing Olivia again was just as he thought it would be. Joy, fear and arousal all rolled into one cruel little package. There was no way he was going to let her out of his sight, so he was glad when she didn't put up a fight about sitting with him. He wanted to spend every second he could with her before she had to get back on that ship.

"So, what exactly brings you to Alaska, Living Doll?" he asked while preparing for takeoff.

"Umm, a cruise ship perhaps?" she joked. "A family vacation, and you know I hated that nickname."

"Still a smart ass I see." He joked back. "Wow, all seven of you? And how can you hate that nickname when a cute, little five year old gave it to you? All I did was continue the usage."

Olivia smiled at the memory. Alex's super cute five year old neighbor had called her a living doll because she'd looked like her toy doll. The resemblance really had been uncanny.

"Let's just get going," damn, she couldn't believe she was actually blushing. The nickname, coming from Alex, didn't bother her nearly as much as it probably should have. She'd actually started liking it toward the end of their relationship.

"Yes ma'am," he stated, giving her a salute. "After the tour could we get together and talk for a bit? Maybe have some lunch?"

Olivia quickly nodded her consent and they were off to Misty Fjord National Monument. Her heart and mind were at war. Her mind was taking in the sheer beauty of what she saw out her window, while thinking up reasons why she shouldn't be there, and her heart was focused on every move and sound Alex made, while aching to be back with him. She settled for just enjoying his presence. She just loved to watch him, she always had. Why couldn't it be sunny, then she could wear her sunglasses and watch him without his knowledge. She could play stalker. Through glimpses she noticed that his dark hair was pretty much the same as it had always been, he still had his perpetual five o'clock shadow and if possible, he was even more muscled, his shoulders broader somehow. He looked so good, delicious really.

Alex was the consummate tour guide and Olivia didn't quite know what to say so she just kept quiet. So much of what she knew she should tell him would be better said alone and not over the headset where the other passengers could hear.

"That my friends is New Eddystone Rock, which is a volcanic plug. If you look closely, you might see eagles perched there," Alex informed the passengers in his perfectly toned tour guide voice. No matter how many times he saw it, he never tired of the majesty of it all.

"How tall is it?" Thomas asked.

"Two hundred thirty four feet." Alex answered in return. "Imagine that!"

This place was definitely beautiful. Olivia loved the waterfalls that appeared out of the sides of tall cliffs, but they were nothing compared to the waterfall at Big Goat Lake. It plunged one-thousand glorious feet. She was in awe, she wanted to crawl inside and get lost in the splendor, with Alex at her side. This Fjord was absolutely the most beautiful place she had ever seen. Her dad had been right, Alaska was well on its way to burying itself deep in her heart.

When the plane landed on a beautiful blue lake, Olivia took in the stillness and beauty that surrounded her.

“Wow!” she whispered

“Peaceful isn’t it?” Alex asked as he grabbed her hand and squeezed it.

“Perfect! Amazing!”

That was something he never expected to hear come out of Olivia’s mouth. Peace and tranquility had never seemed to matter much to her. “There are a lot of places like this here in Alaska,” he said quietly.

She squeezed his hand knowing that the tour was close to being over and she would lose him again. She felt so bad now, she wished she hadn’t agreed to this trip. She should have backed out and let him take Thomas and Vanessa. But then she wouldn’t have been able to enjoy his company this one last time and she would always have wondered *what if*.

Seeing him again for only a few hours and then having to leave him seemed so unfair, but there was nothing she could do about it, because she was only there for one day.

Before long, they were back at the dock and Olivia’s heart started to feel so incredibly heavy. Alex stepped out of the plane to secured it before helping the passengers off, then he went back to retrieve his things, leaving Olivia, Thomas, and Vanessa alone to talk for a moment.

"I'll see you guys at dinner, I think I'm going to spend some time with Alex and do some catching up," she informed them. She just couldn't leave him yet, no matter how many times her brain told her to do so. In the end, she decided that a few hours with him today would be better than never having seen him again at all.

Vanessa hugged her goodbye and whispered in her ear. "Grab on and don't let go this time. He's definitely *The One*"

Olivia shrugged and stepped away to gather her thoughts as Alex handed out the souvenir key chains to the passengers and when she turned back around he was walking toward her.

"I'd like to take you to meet my aunt if you don't mind," he suggested. He found himself staring at her while he waited for her answer. Except for her hair, she hadn't changed much at all, she was still the cutest, sexiest woman he'd ever seen. He was overwhelmed that she was actually there with him.

"I'd like that, I don't think I ever met your aunt, she never came to Vegas. Do I get to see your uncle again too?" she asked.

"He passed away two years ago."

She put a comforting hand on his arm. "I'm so sorry, Alex."

He just nodded, his eyes incredibly sad, and put his hand on the small of her back to steer her toward the office.

His hand felt like white hot fire on her body and she trembled beneath his touch. She thought she could feel him trembling too. It was a relief to know that he was feeling the same things she was.

They walked in comfortable silence for less than five minutes when Alex stopped her in front of a little red building with a lot of windows. “Welcome to Paige Air Tours,” he announced as he took her hand and led her inside.

Olivia shuddered. My goodness, if he didn’t stop touching her she might just turn into a pile of molten lava.

She immediately recognized the older woman sitting behind the counter, it was Pearl from the restaurant. There was something about her smile that said she was a good person. And the sparkle in her eyes told Olivia that spending time with her would be a fun experience.

“Livia, this is Pearl. I never put the word Aunt in front of it though, she tends to get mean.”

“Damn right!” she emphasized. “I’m just Pearl honey.” The older woman walked around the counter to hug her nephew’s long lost love. “I guess it was her wasn’t it Alex.” She pulled back from the hug and took Olivia’s face in her hands “And boy is she a pretty little thing. You never should have let this one go you big dummy.”

“Okay, that’s enough ‘auntie’ Pearl!” Alex quickly jumped out of the way as the older woman pretended to smack him. “I just brought her here to meet you and now I want to show her around town.”

“We met at the diner this morning son. I just wasn’t a hundred percent sure it was her.”

Alex had a look of pure horror on his face when he looked at his aunt. That’s why she had been trying to get him to go over there for breakfast. That sneaky little...he would have to think of a way to get back at her.

Pearl hugged Alex, and then Olivia again. Before his aunt let her go, she whispered to her. “He still loves you,” and then she shooed them out the door.

Olivia followed Alex to his truck and he helped her inside. “Wow, she’s great!” Olivia enthused. Was what Pearl had told her true? Part of her wished it was and part of her hoped it wasn’t. If he still loved her, it would make it even harder to leave at the end of the day. For both of them.

"Yeah, she's pretty great isn't she," Alex agreed as he drove through town pointing out landmarks and other places he obviously loved. His enthusiasm was so contagious it only made Olivia fall more in love with the little seaside community.

"And this," he said, pulling up in front of a small yellow cottage, "is where I live."

"Wow, what a great old house," she exclaimed in awe. She could tell Alex was stunned that she actually seemed to like his home. It wasn't big and fancy, and it wasn't on the lake or a golf course. He was probably really close to going into shock.

"Old is the keyword, but I love it," he stammered. "Would you like to come in for some lunch?"

"I'd love to." Olivia couldn't wait to get a glimpse of his current life. She needed to get some sort of idea about what he had been doing for the last couple of years. As she walked through the front door, she suddenly felt like she was transported into some warm cozy cabin in the woods.

Alex's house was charming. Holy hell, since when had charming been a part of her vocabulary; sophisticated or expensive yeah, but not charming.

"I know it's not what you're used to, but it's home to me," Alex answered as if he had read her thoughts.

"It's great, Alex. It's absolutely perfect."

"Wow," he mumbled, dumbfounded. Either she had changed over the last two years, or she had become a great actress. "Make yourself at home," he said, noticing the tremble in his own voice. He wanted to kiss her so badly, but now wasn't the right time. Not yet, but soon. "So, how does a sandwich and homemade chips sound?"

"Great, I'm famished. Can I help?" she asked.

"No, that's okay. Just make yourself at home. I'll be right back." He disappeared behind a set of swinging doors, into the kitchen.

Olivia walked around his living room looking at some of his Alaskan trinkets. They were so rustic, so charming. There was that word again, *charming*. She decided she liked it.

On display, front and center, on the shelf above his television was the large crystal teddy bear she'd given him on the anniversary of their first date. She knew he had hated it, because it was too materialistic, too expensive for his taste. He never said anything though, he'd just accepted it and put it in the closet, probably because he was afraid that it would break.

It hadn't exactly gone with the décor in his apartment and it really didn't go here in this little house either, so why was it displayed? Her heart pounded and her hands were shaking. Did this mean he missed her, did he still think about her? Could Pearl have been right?

She picked it up off the shelf and walked into the kitchen. "Alex, why did you keep this, and why do you have it on your shelf?"

He put down the knife he held, and turned toward her.

She smiled tentatively at him, waiting for his answer.

After a moment, he walked over to her and took the statue out of her hands, setting it gently on the counter. "Because I missed you," he whispered right before he pulled her close and finally kissed her.

She kissed him back, hard and passionate like it was the only way she could keep breathing. Neither one of them could get enough because it felt like they'd been apart for a lifetime and they needed to make up for it.

They backed out of the kitchen, never breaking their lip lock. And as Alex guided her toward the couch, he slipped her shirt over her head and a moment later, she lifted his from his powerful shoulders. It felt so good to be touching him again. Her hand explored every broad inch of his chest and his muscles jumped beneath her familiar caress. One finger followed the light trail of black hair that ran down his stomach, disappearing beneath his waistband. He groaned and Olivia let her hand slide even lower, running it over the erection straining against his jeans. He grew even harder at the excitement of her touch. He ached for her, three years had been way too long to wait to love her again.

"I missed you too, Alex," she whispered, reaching for the button on his jeans. Her hands shook too much to get them undone, so he reached down to help her and they quickly discarded them together. Dear Lord, he wasn't wearing any underwear, he rarely did when flying, if she remembered correctly. The familiarity of him consumed her. He was ready and waiting for her, exactly like he used to be. Her need threatened to overtake her.

Alex returned the favor as he helped her slip out of her pants, right before they finally reached the couch. The only thing keeping them from being burning skin to burning skin now were her pink lace bra and panties.

He hooked his finger through the thin side of the panties and with one quick tug, they ripped from her body. When he reached up to unhook her bra, she was already disposing of it.

"Still perfect," he hissed. Reaching out for her, he tweaked first one nipple and then the other before dropping his hands to her waist.

Moving slightly closer to him, she brought his hands up to touch her again. He rubbed circles over her firm breasts and then lightly squeezed them. Their eyes locked for a moment and then she offered herself to him. He took one dark nipple into his mouth, tugging, nibbling, and devouring her. Olivia shivered beneath his touch so he did it again.

"God, I missed this." She breathed.

Alex chuckled. "I did too. I missed all of you." He sounded just as breathless as she did. "Is it possible that you're even more beautiful now than you were before?"

Olivia moved away, letting his eyes take her in. Her eyes explored him too, every delectable inch. God, she wanted him in every way imaginable. Immediately.

Impatiently, she pushed him onto the couch and grabbed a throw pillow. Tossing it on the floor, she knelt before him. She wanted to tease him, to taste him again. It had been way too long. Wrapping her hand around his length, she gently squeezed, savoring the feeling of touching him so intimately again. He was pulsing beneath her touch, his body begging for her attention.

"Well, well, look at what we have here," she said as a bead of moisture appeared on the tip.

"Olivia please," he ground out.

"Shh, it's been a long time, just let me do this." She took him into her mouth savoring every sensation. Wrapping her hand around the base, she took turns stroking and teasing him with her tongue. Yes, she really had missed this part of loving him. And by his physical response, he had missed it too. She could feel every pulse as he grew harder between her lips.

"Living Doll, please!" he gently pushed her away. "If I only get to be with you one more time, this is not how I want it to be."

She pulled away and smiled at him. "Spoil sport!"

He chuckled and stood, dragging her to her feet. "Let's go."

"Where are we going?" she almost cried out. Brief disturbing images of him making her leave and go back to the ship entered her mind.

Reaching out to her, he started to stroke, driving her crazy with need. “To the bedroom unless you want to do this on the couch.” He slipped a finger deep inside her, then pulled it back out.

She gasped at the sensation and almost cried at the loss of it when he turned and led her to the back of the house.

“Shit!” He mumbled, stopping mid stride. “I don’t have any condoms in the house. You wouldn’t happen to still be on the pill would you?”

The big smile on her face told him everything he needed to know. She turned to walk back down the hall and he stopped her, wrapping his arms around her waist and raining kisses across her upper back. His hand slipped across her belly and down between her thighs, caressing her until she relaxed enough for him to slip a finger inside. “Seeing you again, touching you again, it feels so much like coming home,” he whispered in her ear.

“Yes!” She shivered and moved back against him as he slipped another finger inside. His other hand searched for the one spot that would bring her home and when he found it, he stroked her relentlessly.

Suddenly feeling hot *and* cold, Olivia knew she was about to lose control. She *wanted* to lose control because she was safe in Alex's arms again. His name slipped from between her lips as her muscles contracted around him and she fell back against his chest, her breath coming in gasps.

Alex held her, stroking her stomach until her breathing slowed to normal. Then he returned to kissing her and teasing her, watching her body come alive again. Her nipples pulled taught and she started to move back against him, whispering his name.

"How about a blast from the past?" he mumbled into her shoulder as he rained kisses across her back. "I don't think I can wait to get you to the bedroom."

"Yes" She knew exactly what he was referring to.

Urgently, he turned her around and backed her up against the wall. "This is like a dream come true."

Olivia's eyes burned with excitement when Alex lifted her up. She wrapped herself around him, accepting the length of him with a familiar sigh, settling onto him as if she had always belonged there.

Alex started to move inside of her, slowly at first and then more urgently. He braced himself with one arm on the wall behind her. He had never needed someone so desperately.

With every thrust Olivia's grip on his shoulders tightened, somehow encouraging him. Her nails dug into his skin, her breasts rubbed against the rough hair on his chest, increasing sensation for the both of them. With every jab of pleasure, Olivia felt herself getting closer to where she wanted to be.

"I'm sorry, Doll," he mumbled

"It's okay, Alex," she whispered. "I'm ready." Her body was starting to pulse and hum.

Alex captured her mouth in a searing kiss, finally toppling over the edge a fraction of a second before she did. In a fog, he lowered her to the ground but refused to let her go. "Can you walk sweetheart?"

"I'm not sure," she laughed. "I think so." She'd pulled away and took a wobbly step down the hallway when he scooped her up and carried her to his bedroom, laying her gently on the king sized four poster bed. He took his rightful place beside her.

"Is it my imagination or was that even better than our first time," Olivia asked.

Alex smiled. "I wanted to make love to you all afternoon." He sounded disappointed.

"There's no way we could have done anything close to that Alex, we've been apart way too long."

"Yeah, I guess you're right," he returned, with another smile. Pulling her closer, he caressed her side. They lay there for a long time, just holding and looking at each other, because they may never be able to again.

It took Alex a while to get up the courage to speak to her. There were so many questions he wanted to ask, so many things he needed to know. There just wasn't going to be enough time – he only had her for a few more hours. His heart ached with every beat and with every second that ticked by on the old Grandfather clock in the living room.

He rolled onto his back. "Olivia?"

"Yeah?"

"Are you happy? Is your life everything you want it to be?" he asked, knowing he probably shouldn't go there yet, if at all.

Olivia took a minute to collect the thoughts that were jumbled in her mind. "I guess so. I mean, I have a great paying job, I'm buying a townhouse, I have good friends, and my brother makes a great roommate."

Running her index finger in circles through the small patch of hair on his chest, she rested her cheek on her other hand so she could see him better. A look crossed his face, but she couldn't read it. The word sorry came to mind though.

"Are you happy Alex?"

"For the most part," he answered. "I love my job, I love where I live, I love being able to go fishing or camping without having to travel too far." He rubbed the side of her breast and she shivered.

It was time for a subject change. She hoped they could make love one more time before she left. All she had to do was make him ready and willing to take another tumble.

She sat up and swung her legs across his hips. Her hands worked up and down across his chest. Her fingers paused to tease his nipples. Bending down, her tongue took over for her fingers and she elicited a groan from him. She moved up to press her lips to his and felt him growing hard against her backside. His hands kneaded her thighs and worked up her body until they captured her breasts. She writhed above him.

Alex rolled her over, tucking her beneath him, and started slowly kissing his way down her body, stopping to pay close attention to each breast and trail kisses across her tanned, flat stomach.

Spreading her beautiful thighs, he kissed and nibbled the inside of each one before spreading her open to find her pleasure spot, flicking it with his tongue. She lifted her hips wanting more, and he obliged, first with his tongue and then with his fingers. While his hand stayed below, he kissed his way back up her body until he reached her mouth. She tasted herself on his lips as she returned his kiss, and their passion exploded. He sensed that only a few more caresses would cause her to lose control, but he wasn't ready to take her there quite yet, so he backed off and watched as her hands instinctively moved to where his had been. "Maybe I'll just lay here and watch you. I always loved seeing you please yourself."

"No Alex! Please!" she gasped. "Not this time. I need to feel you inside of me again. Now." She pushed him onto his back and straddled him once again, lowering herself slowly, savoring every last inch. Oh how exquisite, why couldn't this last forever?

Grabbing her hips, Alex helped her rise and fall to fully engulf him with every downward motion. He wanted more, now and forever. He pushed deeper into her until she cried out. How would he ever go on without this, without her? He increased his speed as she increased hers, trying to make the most of every second. Olivia threw her head back and began the all too familiar tremble of impending climax. With each hard stab of pleasure, each sound of flesh against flesh, she felt herself losing control. She wanted to hold on, she tried to hold on, to suspend time, but with one final gasp, she closed in around him and he followed her to the most satisfying, yet heartbreaking finish of their lives.

Olivia collapsed against Alex and he held her tight, never wanting to let her go. But reality intruded as it always did, and he reluctantly got up and started pulling clothes from his dresser. "Go get your clothes while I make you something to eat," he agonized as he dressed. A few minutes later he was gone and Olivia felt lonelier than she ever had.

Forcing herself out of the bed, she went into the other rooms to gather her clothes. The first thing she grabbed were her ruined panties. Remembering how Alex had torn them from her, she felt her entire body flush. She couldn't help but wish that she could have just a few more hours with him, leaving him was going to be the most awful thing she'd ever had to do.

Minus the panties she quickly dressed and sat down at the dining table.

"Here we go, some soup and some hot tea. The sandwiches were a bit stale when I got back in there." Alex smiled at her and placed the food on the table in front of her.

She laughed "Thank you, it's perfect."

He loved hearing her laugh again. “Can I ask you something, Livia?”

“Sure,” she said as she savored a spoonful of soup. It was absolutely delicious, one of his famous homemade dishes obviously.

“Earlier, when I asked you if you were happy, you didn’t say you loved anything in your life. Do you, love anything I mean?”

His question served as a reminder of how different their lives were and probably always would be. Sure, she sometimes questioned her career choice and she was sometimes bored with her social circle, but that didn’t mean she was ready to give up the life she had built for herself.

She knew that was what Alex was getting at, he wanted to prove to her that her lifestyle was wrong, and maybe that she should give it up to be with him. As much as she cared for him and wanted to spend a little more time here, she didn’t want to actually change. She just couldn’t. Period. End of story.

“Alex, I don’t think we should talk about this. My life is fine, yours is fine. Let’s just leave it at that.” The three hardest sentences she would ever utter.

“If that’s what you want,” he whispered. “When you’re done with your soup I’ll take you back to the ship." He'd been prepared to fight for her, but now for some reason, his fight was gone.

"I'm done, I guess we should go now."

"Okay." He answered.

The ride to the dock wasn't a pleasant one. The tension was thicker than the fog that rolls in off the ocean. Neither of them had the courage to say much of anything so they rode along in awkward silence. When Alex stopped the truck, he reached over and grabbed her hand. "Today meant a lot to me Olivia, if you ever need anything, you know where to find me."

"Thank you." A bittersweet smile crossed her face. "Today meant a lot to me too."

"Give me your phone, Doll," Alex demanded.

She didn't question it, she just handed it over. He typed something into hers and then something into his and handed it back.

He leaned over and kissed her gently. "Goodbye again, Olivia."

"Goodbye Alex," she whispered. She hopped down out of the truck and sprinted across the street and when she turned to wave goodbye, he was next to his vehicle waving back at her.

Olivia made it across the gangplank and through security before the tears came and she was blissfully alone in the elevator as it climbed to deck six. She headed straight to her brother's cabin but he wasn't there. Thomas let her in and left her in peace, crying on her brother's bed.

She didn't quite understand why she was crying, it was her decision to keep her current life, it was the life she wanted...the life she refused to give up. One day of passion and old memories wasn't enough to change that, to change her.

Chapter 5

Olivia finally cried herself out, got up off of Jackson's bed and headed back to her own cabin. She would catch up with her twin later. It was formal night and they were taking family pictures so she had to make sure she looked perfect or her mother dear would freak the hell out. Why did it have to be tonight of all nights though? She wasn't quite sure how she would survive, but she had to try. The last thing she needed was the sympathy and/or disapproving eye of her meddling mother.

Mari was in the shower when Olivia made it back to the cabin and Vanessa walked in right behind her. "How did it go Sis?" Vanessa asked, taking in Olivia's red, splotchy face.

"Just like old times," she answered sarcastically. "Every last bit of it. From the great sex to the great food to the *big* disagreement about lifestyles." Somehow Olivia kept the tears at bay even when her sister hugged her tight.

"Maybe you can find some sort of closure now?" Vanessa hoped so, only for her sister's sake. She actually wished Alex had locked her stubborn sibling in his basement.

"Yeah, maybe," Olivia whispered. "I'm going to take a shower after Mari, okay."

"Can I take one first, please?" Vanessa begged. "I want to meet Thomas for drinks before dinner."

"Come on Nessa, I really need to try to wash some of this emotional day away."

They were in a full blown argument over who would shower next when Mari stepped into the room. It was then decided that Olivia would shower while make-up expert Vanessa helped Mari prepare to finalize the seduction of her soon to be ex-husband,

Olivia made the shower as hot as she could stand it. Stepping under the spray felt so good and so bad at the same time. Her stress started to seep away just a bit, but as she washed herself, the last vestiges of Alex swirled down the drain. Every touch, every kiss, every pleasure he'd plied her body with disappeared and all she had left were the memories of their time together. It seemed memories were all she was ever meant to have of him.

****

Watching Olivia walk away again was killing Alex. He wanted to block the ship and not let it leave until she agreed to stay with him, but of course that wasn't possible. He had no idea what to do or where to go now. He felt lost. Again.

Getting into his truck, he just started driving with no real destination in mind. His heart broke more with every second. Via a roundabout route, he found himself pulling up to the office. Pearl's car was parked out front and he was actually relieved that she was still there. He knew he could always talk to her, her advice might be a bit eccentric at times, but it was usually good.

The bell above the door rang as he wandered in and Pearl looked up from her desk. She immediately knew that something was wrong.

"What happened?"

"Everything, and then nothing, she went back to the ship, never to see the likes of me again."

"I'm sorry," Pearl sympathized.

"Thanks," he said sighing. "You know Pearl, I thought I saw signs of change in her. She isn't as materialistic and she actually seemed to enjoy being outside, experiencing nature. I thought for sure we would have a shot again, that maybe we could compromise a life together." He sat down on the edge of her desk and sighed again. "I guess I was wrong, I never should have even hoped..."

"If you saw signs of change, I'm sure they were really there," Pearl advised.

Alex thought about that for a few minutes. "You know, you're right! The signs were there. Hell, she actually liked my little old house. But at the last minute, she just closed up saying our lives are fine the way they are."

"*At the last minute* are the key words Alex. I think she's still in the process of changing her life, but she doesn't want to admit it yet. Maybe she doesn't even know that it's happening." Pearl made him look her in the eyes. "She's afraid Alex, you need to show her that there isn't anything to be afraid of."

"Yeah, and how in the hell do I do that when she lives in the lower forty-eight and I live up here. I won't go back there Pearl, ever!" He had to calm himself, it wouldn't do any good to yell at his aunt.

"We'll have to think of a plan," she said.

"Good luck with that one Pearl."

Alex stood and walked behind his desk, grabbing a stack of paperwork to look over. Maybe that would keep his mind occupied for a while.

Pearl interrupted him when he was halfway through the stack of supply invoices that he really didn't remember reading. "I've got it, Alex. I know how you can see her again."

"I've *got* to hear this," he said skeptically.

"You take one of the planes and you follow her to her ports of call. Show her that you love her and that she loves you, the change will come on its own."

"I can't do that Pearl, I have a business to run."

"Yes you can. Who do you think helped your uncle run this place before you showed up? Who trained you?" she reminded him. "I'll handle the business and Jason and Mark will handle the flights."

"I don't know Pearl, I don't think Jason and Mark would agree. This is our busy season."

Pearl shook her head at her stubborn nephew. "Yes they would. I called them while you had your head buried in that stack of papers pretending to work. It's all set. All you have to do is pack a bag and head for the next port."

Alex was still skeptical, but he was also getting excited. "I don't know Pearl. I can't just leave you alone here. It wouldn't be fair."

"You'll do it, or I'll keep the house," she threatened.

"You wouldn't."

"Try me, Alex!"

Oh man, she was serious. This could work though. Hell, he had to try, he couldn't just sit there doing nothing. He wanted her back and he wasn't going to rest until he had her.

Hugging his aunt, he whispered, "Thank you Auntie Pearl." He braced himself for what was to come, and nothing happened, for once she didn't even pretend to hit him.

"Get on out of here, Alex. Go get her and bring her back to be a part of our family."

Alex stood and headed to the door when Pearl called him back. "What ship is she on?" she asked him.

"The *Sunset Destiny*. Why?"

"It might help to have the itinerary if you want to know where you are flying to."

Alex laughed. "Yeah, that might be a good idea."

Pearl handed him the sheet she printed off and he ran out of the office. A quick trip home to pack a bag, and he was on his way to Skagway.

****

Olivia never thought of herself as a good actress, but at family pictures and formal night dinner she could have won an Academy Award. She smiled when it was expected and posed like everyone else. On the outside, she was the usual happy go lucky Olivia, but on the inside, she was dying a slow, painful, emotional death.

At dinner, everyone was in high spirits so Olivia played along. She even cracked jokes and laughed with the group. She did have to admit that Mari's excitement, over what she was about to do with Graham, was catching so she didn't have to try too hard sometimes.

By the time dessert arrived, she was feeling a bit better, buoyed by Mari's excitement and her own seething anger at her mother. An anger that would be released as soon as dinner was over. She couldn't wait!

"So, what are we going to do tonight Sis?" Jackson asked as they left the dining room. "Maybe go out for drinks? That guy you met last night said he'd be at the bar."

Olivia hadn't told her brother about seeing Alex and probably wouldn't yet. The subject was too painful right now. The emotions were more raw than they'd been when she first stepped foot back on the ship. But that meant she couldn't beg off hanging out with him at the bar without creating suspicion and a lot of questions.

"Yeah, the bar sounds great." She faked enthusiasm well. "We'll go after I have a chat with mother, I'll meet you there in thirty minutes."

Jackson kissed his twin on the cheek. "Go easy on her Livia, I have a sneaking suspicion I know what this is all about, and she only wants to help."

Olivia glared at her brother and smacked his chest. "Her kind of help only hurts." She walked away and headed back to the dining room to wait for her mother to emerge. When she finally did, she had Graham's little daughter in tow.

"Mother I need to have a word with you," Olivia demand.

"Of course dear," she said sweetly. "Eleanor can take Sarah to the kids program and I'll meet her at the Sail Away lounge when we're done."

Olivia kept a close eye on her mother to see if she showed any fear or remorse or any other kind of similar emotion, but all Olivia saw was a certain smugness in her smile. Her anger started to grow.

"So, how was your trip over Misty Fjord dear?" Charlotte asked. "I hope I picked the perfect tour for you."

"You know damn well how the trip was mother." Olivia couldn't control her anger.

"Whatever do you mean dear?" Charlotte asked, her voice dripping with innocence.

Yuck! "Give it up mother," Olivia cried. "You know damn well that you sent me on that excursion to run into Alex. Don't even try to deny it."

"You ran into Alex? My, oh my, how is he doing?" Charlotte asked as if she didn't already know. "I always did love that boy."

"Don't give me that shit!" Olivia ground out. "We all know damned well what you are up to. Enough is enough Mother, before someone gets hurt."

Charlotte looked at her daughter with a bit of pride. Her children didn't usually stand up to her. "You know I only do what's best for you kids," she finally stated. A roundabout admission if nothing else. "No one will get hurt. Just look at Mari and Graham. They are so happy and they are going to have the best night of their lives tonig..."

Olivia interrupted. "And then what mother? Graham doesn't want a relationship. Period. End of story. When this all blows up in a couple of days, Mari is going be hurting more than she was before." Olivia sighed and started walking to the elevator.

Charlotte followed her.

"And what about me mother? How am I supposed to move on after today? I've now lost Alex twice in one lifetime." Tears were starting to fall and Olivia quickly wiped them away.

Charlotte grabbed her daughter in a tight embrace. Olivia didn't struggle free but she didn't hug back either. "I wouldn't have done this if I thought anyone would get hurt, *in the end.*" Charlotte released her. "You know, this doesn't have to be losing Alex again. You know where he is now, the rest is up to you." She turned and walked away leaving Olivia gaping after her.

****

"Hey, is everything okay?" Jackson asked as he walked out of the Ocean Wave Lounge to meet Olivia.

"I saw Alex today," was all she said as she walked into the bar to find a table.

Jackson followed her. “I had a feeling,” he stated. “I didn’t know what Charlotte had planned until after she asked me to bring Alex up in conversation a lot.” Jack calling their mother by her first name meant he was angry with her too.

“And of course you did as she asked right?” Olivia seethed.

Jackson sighed and looked into his sister’s sad eyes. “I’m sorry Livia, she bribed me. Not that it clicked right away, but once I saw what was going on with the others, I knew.” He smiled. “I was going to warn you if that makes you feel any better.”

“Good Lord, why didn’t you?”

“Would it have made a difference?” he asked. “Would you have stayed away?”

Olivia sighed. “No.” If she’d found out that Alex was in Ketchikan before they’d docked, her first instinct would have been to run or hide. But then she would have sought him out. Because she’d missed him that much. Because she’d never stopped loving him.

Jackson just nodded. “So, how is he?”

“Happy, except for missing me,” Olivia told him.

“You miss him too?” It was stated as a question.

"Yes, very much," she managed to choke out.

"Yet, by the way you're acting, you cut him off again." Jackson accused.

"It's no use, we live in different worlds. Everything is just too confusing to deal with. It's time to finally move on."

Jackson hugged his sister. All he could do now was support her. He'd tried many times to talk sense into her, always with negative results. In reality, his twin wasn't the bitch everyone thought she was. She was just afraid, afraid of the unknown. This fear gave her a warped sense of what she wanted out of life. Any change was up to her and Alex now.

"Hey, do you want to hear what's been going on with me?" he asked, to change the subject. "I think I'm ready to talk now!"

"Yes! What's going on baby brother?"

"Baby brother? You're only ten minutes older."

"Still older, now spill it!"

Jackson grimaced and started his tale. "They think Deborah is in Anchorage or maybe Denali."

"What!" Jackson's first love had disappeared when they were sixteen, without a word to anyone.

"Yeah, I got a call from her mom the other day. She's been searching for her in

Alaska for about four years now. She found out she'd been living near Denali National Park with her reclusive uncle."

"But why?" Olivia asked. She couldn't even imagine.

"She was apparently in some kind of danger, we don't know the whole story yet," he sighed. "But damn it, I'm gonna find out!"

"You still miss her don't you?"

"Yes, but that's not the whole story, Livia." His voice became shaky and he turned away from his sister.

"Jackson, look at me."

He turned to her but averted his gaze. "I have a son, Livia. His name is Michael. If I can't find Deb, I have to bring him home because Deb's mom is his guardian and she's dying of cancer." He had tears in his eyes. "Can you believe it, I'm a dad!"

Olivia wrapped her arms around her twin. "How scary, exciting and wonderful!" she cried. "I can't wait to meet my nephew."

Jackson smiled at her. "I'm so glad you understand. But you can't tell anyone, and when I tell the family, you have to pretend you never knew."

"I'll be the best actress ever, no one will know," she promised. After all, she'd just put on the performance of a lifetime at dinner.

Jackson looked up toward the doorway. "Your new friend Steven is headed this way. I think I'll leave you two alone. Please just promise me you won't do something you'll regret."

"I'll try not to, that's all I can promise you."

Jackson kissed her forehead and walked out of the lounge.

"Hey beautiful," Steven said as he approached.

"Hi Steven."

"What are you drinking tonight?" he asked her.

"Something strong," she answered.

"Be right back."

A few minutes later, he returned with a drink she had never had before. She didn't even want to know what it was, as long as it was strong and oh boy was it ever. It burned her throat going down and hopefully it would burn away her hurt for a while too. At least she had Steven for company, to keep her mind off of Alex. The twenty-seven year old entertainment publicist was funny and engaging and she enjoyed talking to him.

They were drinking and talking about their day in Ketchikan when it was announced that there would be dancing there in the lounge. Olivia was disappointed, she only liked dancing with Alex.

"I don't feel like dancing, what should we do?" Olivia asked.

"I don't know," he answered.

"Well, we need to get out of here, that's for sure," Olivia noted. "It's getting crowded.

Steven finished his drink and set his glass on the table. "I have an idea, did you bring a swimsuit?"

"Yeah, I did. Why?" she asked curiously.

"Hot tub!"

"Great idea, I'll meet you at the one on deck nine in fifteen minutes," she said as she finished her drink and stood to leave. After the day she'd had, a soak in the hot tub sounded great.

While Olivia waited at the elevator, she saw Mari and Graham going into the dance at the Ocean Breeze. Maybe they were going dancing before making love for the first time, it was all quite romantic. Alex was romantic too. He was a great dancer, and a great lover for that matter. But that was over now. A hot tub and a very sexy new man awaited.

Boy she wished her sisters were in the cabin, she needed their advice, bikini or one piece, which should she chose? Steven would probably appreciate the bikini more, and it was more comfortable so she went with it. It was time to have fun and forget about Alex.

"Hey Steven, sorry I'm late," Olivia said as she reached the hot tub.

"No problem, I haven't been here long myself."

Olivia took off her wrap and stepped into the swirling hot water. "Oh this feels fantastic," she exclaimed, settling in next to Steven.

"You *look* fantastic," he said.

She smiled at him, it wasn't the first time she'd heard that, but she liked hearing it all the same.

Leaning back, she felt her muscles relax and she closed her eyes. For the first time all night, her mind was relatively clear and she felt somewhat normal.

"Hey, don't fall asleep on me." Steven said laughing.

Opening her eyes, she smiled at him. "Don't worry, I won't. I guess the hot water mixed with alcohol, on a relatively empty stomach, is relaxing me a little too much. I probably should have eaten more at dinner." She looked at Steven, noticing for the first time just how handsome he was. She recognized the look in his eyes too, it bordered on hunger, and not the kind that would be sated by food.

"Can I kiss you, Olivia?" he asked.

"Yes," she whispered.

He reached for her and kissed her lightly. His hand caressed her side under the water, slowly making its way to the side of her breast.

Her body stiffened and she gently pushed him away. This wasn't right. She had just been with Alex, she should still be with Alex.

"I'm sorry, I can't do this. I'm sorry if I led you on." She took a deep breath, looking away from him. "I guess I just have some pretty heavy stuff I need to deal with right now." Standing, she stepped out of the hot tub, grabbed her wrap and quickly walked away. "Damn it mother, how could you do this to me," she mumbled to herself.

Olivia felt so guilty, she never should have gone out with Steven. He probably thought she was some insane lunatic and she was leaning toward that thought herself. She didn't really know what to think about everything that had happened that day. All she knew was that being in Alex's arms that afternoon made her feel more at ease than she had in a long, long time.

She suddenly needed to hear his voice again, but Ketchikan was long gone. There was no turning back. But she was pretty sure he'd put his number in her phone. She didn't care how high the roaming charges would be, she needed to call him.

She raced back to her cabin and dug her phone out of her bag. She searched her contacts and there was Alex's number. She hit call.

"Hello Doll," he answered on the second ring.

"Hi Alex." She sat there, not quite knowing what to say next.

"Is everything okay?" he asked, getting concerned by her silence.

"Yeah, yeah, everything's fine." She responded. "I guess I just wanted to apologize for snapping at you earlier. I could have handled that so much better."

"It's okay Livia, I was being too pushy. You had every right to snap at me."

Olivia sighed. "I'm still sorry."

"I know."

"Alex, I'm sorry if it leads you on, but I just need to say this." She paused.

"Go ahead, Livia."

"I really miss you," she whispered just loud enough for him to hear.

"I really miss you too. You know, anytime you want to talk, just call or text. I'll be here."

"I'd like that, Alex. It would be nice to stay in touch," she confirmed.

"I'd like that too."

"I've got to go now, Alex. I'll call you again soon."

"Okay Livia. I..."

"Alex?" When he didn't answer, she looked at her phone and noticed she'd lost signal. She knew nothing good could come from staying in touch with him, but she just couldn't help herself.

Three hours later she woke when her phone buzzed. She'd fallen asleep holding it. When she checked the screen, the signal had finally come back and there was a text from Alex. It said *...still love you.* Olivia didn't know whether to cry or smile. She fell back to sleep quickly, with a smile on her face and tears in her eyes.

Chapter 6

Olivia slept well despite the thoughts of Alex that invaded her sleep. She felt somewhat at peace with her decision to stay in touch with him. It would be hard, but much better than never speaking to him again. Lord knows, she would probably never make it back to Ketchikan so the phone would be their lifeline to a continued friendship.

That thought made her sad though. She would love to have had a bit more time to be with him in his cute little house. She wanted to meet his friends, and go to his favorite hangouts. Getting to know his Aunt Pearl would be a riot too, she just knew they could be great friends. But then the voice of reason chimed in reminding her of the custom home on the golf course that she had her eye on, and the fact that Alex was just a tour pilot. And then a conflicting voice asked her if it all even mattered that much. She was finally so frustrated and confused that she got out of bed. It was only six a.m.

Dressed in a warm sweat suit, she quietly left the room and headed for the outdoor track. A long run in the forty degree air would do her good. With so many conflicting thoughts, she would probably have to run five-hundred miles. Whether it would clear her mind or not remained to be seen.

After a mile, she finally felt sufficiently numb, and hungry, so she decided to return to the room. She was still off kilter, but the tension was taken down a notch or two. Her sister hadn't even stirred by the time she made it back to the cabin and showered. When she was finally standing in front of the mirror, brushing her hair, she heard Vanessa's sleepy voice behind her.

"When is the train trip in Skagway?"

"Good morning sleepy head! The excursion is in a few hours I think," Olivia answered.

"I suppose I should get up." But Vanessa didn't move. She wanted info on Olivia's afternoon with Alex and *then* she would get up. "So, what happened with lover boy yesterday?"

Olivia sighed and sat down next to her sister. "He introduced me to his Aunt, he showed me around town and then he took me back to his place."

"Did he take you there for lunch, or *dessert*?" she asked jokingly.

"Both," Olivia said not looking at her sister. "I mean we had both, but I don't think *dessert* is the specific reason he took me there."

"I see. And you are so sad because he was awful in bed? I mean, because dessert was so awful?"

Olivia swatted at her sister, and smiled brightly. "No, the sex was great, it always was. I'm just missing him, that's all."

"Well, if you miss him, then go be with him. It's a no brainer Liv."

"It's not that easy Nessa. I wish it were. I just don't think I can live peacefully within his world."

"Well, that's a good sign," Vanessa said happily. "You used to say that you *knew* you couldn't live within his world, and now you only *think* you can't. I'd say there is still hope for you two."

Olivia just shook her head and got up from the bed. "I don't think so little sister." Tears choked her voice. "We'll stay in touch through phone and text, but that's as far as it'll go. I'll probably never see him again." She went through her phone and found the message from Alex and tossed the device to her sister. “And then there’s this.”

Vanessa read it and tossed the phone back. “Wow. I personally think it’s great that he still loves you. How do you feel about it?”

Olivia looked at her sister and shrugged. “It’s sweet.” Then she disappeared into the bathroom with tears shining in her eyes.

Vanessa let Olivia wander off. She didn’t want to make her sister cry, she just wanted to talk, or knock, some sense into her, somehow, someway, someday.

Olivia sat on the toilet seat to get her bearings and her phone rang. “Hello,” she answered breathlessly.

“Hey, Doll.”

“How are you today?” Olivia asked

“I’m good, you?” Alex returned.

“Good, sitting in the bathroom to have some alone time. The joys of a small cabin, you know.””

Alex laughed. “I can imagine. Did you get my text?” he asked.

“I did!” Olivia answered with a bit too much enthusiasm.

Alex chuckled. “That’s good, I hope you slept well.”

“I did, we had a busy day yesterday.”

"That we did," Alex agreed. "What do you have planned for today?"

"The whole family is going on some sort of a train trip. It's supposed to be a great excursion."

"It is!" Alex enthused. "I've been on it before. If you loved the flight tour yesterday you'll love the train."

"Oh good, I'm sure I'll enjoy it if it's half as beautiful as yesterday's tour."

"Call me when you're done and tell me what you thought of it." He paused for a minute. "Can I ask you a question Livia?"

"Of course." She really hoped she wouldn't regret it.

"Do you still miss me?"

She laughed in relief. "Absolutely."

"I miss you too." They were both silent for a while.

"I, I guess I should go Alex, it's almost time for breakfast."

"Okay, I'll talk to you after your trip."

"Bye Alex."

"Bye Love."

Olivia left the bathroom and climbed up onto her bunk. She loved that she could now talk to Alex whenever she wanted to. Her phone buzzed in her hand and she knew it was a text from him. And she knew exactly what it would say. *I still love you.*

Olivia and Vanessa were discussing breakfast when Mari burst into the room and they descended on her, asking questions about losing her virginity and finally getting Graham after twelve years of wanting him, but all she would say was that she wouldn't tell tales about the man she was spending the rest of her life with. It seemed Charlotte's plan had worked with Mari and Graham. They received further confirmation when Mari came out of the bathroom after her shower and packed her bags.

"Whoa, wait a minute, where are you going?" Vanessa asked her sister.

"I'm moving in with my husband, did you not hear what I said earlier?"

"It's true then, that's all it took. All you had to do to make him love you was to have sex with him?" Olivia asked incredulous.

"Mind blowing sex and a *lot* of talking…"

Olivia tuned out the rest of what her sisters talked about. Charlotte had actually succeeded in getting a pair together so now they would all be in for more matchmaking hell. Her mother would feel invincible now.

Her heart suddenly ached. Why the hell couldn't it have been her and Alex? But then again Graham and Mari lived in the same general area and wanted the same things out of life whereas she and Alex lived worlds apart, not only in miles but in lifestyle. Her reverie was interrupted by a knock on the door. Graham had come to rescue his wife from her intrusive sisters.

Olivia and Vanessa had plans to do some shopping in Skagway before the family train trip so shortly after Mari left, they grabbed muffins and juice for breakfast and headed into town.

"So how are you and Thomas doing?" Olivia asked as they left the ship.

"Don't ask."

"That bad huh?"

"Yeah, you could say that," Vanessa lamented, looking up at the towering mountains that surrounded the town. "We fight every day, but I can't resist being with him. Aside from being frustrating as hell, he can be sweet, exciting and funny too."

"And the sex?" Olivia questioned.

"Unbelievable," Vanessa gushed. "So much better than our first time when we were teens."

Olivia laughed because her infallible sister was actually blushing! "Sounds like love to me Nessa."

"I don't know about that…Yet," she returned, refusing to talk anymore about it and quickening her pace.

Olivia decided to leave her sister alone for the time being. As she tried in vain to keep up with her long legged sibling, she took a good look around and decided that she liked Skagway, it was a really nice little town. Although, it was a bit overrun by tourists. Even this early in the day, the streets were packed with cruise ship passengers. Still, they walked from crowded shop to crowded shop, for over an hour, admiring the charming old buildings that spoke of the Gold Rush history of Alaska. Tall snow covered peaks surrounded the town and Olivia decided she liked them. She'd never realized how beautiful, how peaceful mountains could be. They made her feel safe somehow.

"Hey look, I think maybe I'll bring Thomas on this saloon tour," Vanessa enthused, pointing to a sign on a nearby building. "He'll love the authentic characters that are portrayed by townspeople. Especially if they have saloon girls." The excitement showed in her eyes.

"I thought you guys were fighting," Olivia pointed out.

"Minor detail." She winked at her sister. "Come on, we need to get going so we don't' miss the family excursion.

When they finally reached the train, everybody but Mari, Graham, Eleanor and

Sarah were there. Charlotte excused herself and walked over to talk with one of the tour employees.

"What's going on?" Olivia asked Ethan as Vanessa practically skipped over to hug Thomas.

"They can't find room for all of us on the same car even though when we made the reservation they said we would be able to travel together," he informed the group which now included Graham, Mari, and Sarah.

Olivia looked at her glowing big sister. Even though she was jealous, she couldn't help but be happy for them. They always had been and always would be the perfect couple. She couldn't understand why her twin was practically glaring at them. He had to be happy for them, they all loved the Blake family after all. But her brother had been a real hot head lately, and she just hoped he didn't cause trouble. He had that troublemaker look in his eyes.

"Okay everybody, we've got a plan now so everyone can stay together," Ethan yelled over the noise. "It turns out there are only two people on the wheelchair accessible car and they have agreed to share their space with us so we can be together. We board in five minutes."

****

The train trudged slowly along the tracks through town but soon picked up speed. Once they were clear and on a steady path, passengers were allowed to roam around the train and step out on the platforms that separated each car. Olivia decided to stay seated and watch the scenery go by through the tall windows to her right. A Gold Rush cemetery was the first thing that caught her eye. How fascinating to think of the history that existed there. Those men, from so long ago, with so many stories of hardship, happiness and heartbreak.

The farther they traveled, the more scenic the route became. Waterfalls appeared in the sides of cliffs, mountains and glaciers towered far above, and when the river became visible, Olivia wanted to suspend time to listen to it rushing past.

The scenery brought thoughts of Alex and she smiled. She had finally started to enjoy and appreciate the great outdoors, and now she would probably forever equate it with him, they would become synonymous.

She really did miss him. How she could miss him even more now, in one day, than she had over the last three years? She decided she would probably be trying to answer that question for a long time to come. Staying in touch with him probably wouldn't help either, but it was something she just had to do. Her life plan would probably never bring her near Ketchikan again, so she had to accept that she had *seen* Alex for the last time, and her dear mother would have to accept it too. Charlotte could never know that she was staying friends with him or the matchmaking would never end until they were both dead and buried with broken hearts.

When the train turned around and headed back to Skagway, Olivia decided to get up and walk around, maybe check out the view from a different vantage point. She even contemplated going outside to see if she could see one of the waterfalls coming out of the cliffs up close and personal. She wanted to see if it was possible to feel the spray on her face.

At the door of the train car, Olivia looked out and saw Mari and Graham together. They looked so happy, so in love. She didn't want to interrupt their togetherness. Besides, it was too painful to see their happiness. She would love see the beauty and be able to feel the spray of the water, all while wrapped in Alex's arms.

Olivia turned around and walked back to stand at the window to rest her forehead against the cool glass. Alex would be so proud of her, she was actually enjoying the great outdoors, she actually noticed the beauty and details of what she saw, she noticed and understood a bit about how beautiful life truly was now. Before, she'd heard the birds in the trees, and knew they were there, but now she knew to look up and notice the birds perched and singing on the fragile looking branches.

The door from the outside opened and she moved to take her turn on the platform. She saw Graham helping Mari into a seat and her sister was scarily pale.

"Mari, sweetie are you okay?" Olivia called out as she rushed to her sister's side.

"She almost fell off the train, Livia," Graham informed her. "Can you sit with her while I go talk to my mom?"

"Of course!" Olivia sat and wrapped her arms around her big sister. She comforted Mari as best she could and let her talk out her fears until she finally asked Olivia to take her back to her husband.

Jackson motioned his twin over, with concern in his eyes. "What's going on?" he asked.

"Mari fell, but Graham caught her." Olivia was shaking so bad she felt like she should probably sit down again.

Ethan walked up to them after having talked with the couple.

"Dad are they okay?" Olivia asked.

"Yeah, they're fine, but you don't look so good. Jackson, take your sister over there to sit down. I'm going to let everyone know there is nothing to worry about now."

"Yes sir," Jackson answered his father. He took Olivia to a seat and dropped down beside her. "Are you okay sis?"

"Yeah, I'm fine," she whispered. "They just found each other again, what if they had lost it all. It's so scary to think about."

"It makes you want to hold onto the one you love doesn't it?" Jackson surmised.

She knew he was talking about Alex. Why couldn't her brother understand that she just couldn't do anything about her and Alex? For her, there were more important things in life than love – stability and peace of mind were two big ones and she had those. She didn't want to talk about it, or even think about it. She didn't want the hassle of thinking about anything else. "Don't Jack, not right now."

"You're remembering the hike aren't you?"

Olivia shivered. "Yeah," she mumbled.

About a year before she and Alex broke up, a whole group of them had gone out to Valley of Fire State Park to hang out and party before the temperatures got too high. As usual when they were in the great outdoors, she and Alex started to fight. They didn't want to disturb the party, so they hiked away from the group. Alex started climbing some rocks and Olivia followed him. She wasn't the best at climbing but of course she had to say her piece. Before she knew it they were high above the desert, looking down at their friends, joking around and having fun. Olivia remembered telling Alex he needed to get his act together because he'd mentioned how he wished he could hike for a living. And he had been offended and accused her of not understanding him. The argument continued as they looked across the desert from above. It was all stuff they'd argued about before, it was almost as if they recited it from a script on cue by then. But that one time, Alex veered from the script. Olivia remembered it vividly, even years later, the only time Alex had ever uttered something mean to her. "Sometimes I don't know why I ever fell in love with you." *The words stung so badly that all she wanted to do was escape. When she twirled around to flee, the rocks beneath her crumbled and she felt herself falling. She reached out in desperation and her hands grasped a ledge but she could feel it crumbling under her fingers. She cried out to Alex and he appeared at the ledge, grabbed her arms and pulled her safely back to the center of the rock.* "I'm so sorry Livia, I didn't mean it." *He'd said it as he held onto her shaking body. It had brought them closer for a while, they had really worked hard on their relationship until Alex quit job number twelve in two years. That was the beginning of the end for them.*

Alex had saved her life just as Graham had saved Mari's. For the first time ever, Olivia realized how hard she'd been on him, how many times *her* words must have stung *him*. She wasn't ready to change her life by any means, but she could at least try to make things up to him. Why he still loved her, she couldn't understand. There wasn't much she could remember, at that point, that had been loveable.

The train pulled into the depot and Jackson got up to join their father for a planned hike and Olivia headed toward the exit.

Vanessa pulled her aside. "Hey, you want to come with Thomas and me? We're going to tour saloons."

"No thanks, I think I'm going to take it easy. Mari's fall scared the crap out of me.

She didn't mention that the memory of the hike was eating her alive and it made her feel better to wallow in the guilt.

She'd promised to let Alex know about the train excursion so as she blindly followed her sister off the train, she hit the speed dial she'd set for him.

"Hi Doll," he answered on the fourth ring. The sound of his voice cheered her immediately.

"Hi Alex. I'm about to leave the train. You were right, the trip was wonderful."

"I thought you'd like it. What are you doing now?" he asked.

"Heading back to the ship, or maybe just walking around town. What are you doing?"

"Standing here, looking at the most beautiful woman in the world," he nearly whispered.

An ache started in her heart and spread through her body. Alex was already with someone else?

"Look up, Livia."

When she raised her head she saw her family gathered around someone. And then she saw him. It was Alex, holding his phone to his ear. She was the woman he'd been talking about. What in the hell was he doing there? She had everything planned out. She'd call him, text him, make things up to him and never see him again. Or so she'd thought.

Her family seemed almost as happy to see him as she actually was. She wouldn't let him see how happy she was though, she really couldn't afford to. There was no reason to lead him on any more than she already was with their phone calls. As she approached him, her family seemed to fade into the background even though they were all still standing there next to him. They both put their phones away.

"Hi, Living Doll."

"Hi, what the hell are you doing here?" It was highly annoying that her voice sounded more breathless than angry.

"I came to see if you wanted to go for a hike."

"What if I have other plans? I didn't know you would be here." She didn't have plans of course. She was actually very happy to see him, but it threw her whole world off kilter and she didn't like it one bit. And to top it off, she realized that most likely he was already in Skagway when he'd called her that morning.

Alex just shrugged, flashing that devastatingly handsome smile of his and took his phone back out of his pocket and typed something into it.

Olivia's phone buzzed and she checked the message. It said *I still love you.* It didn't matter though, he was still being presumptuous and slightly deceitful. And then Charlotte just had to speak up. "You don't have any plans sweetie. Go with him, he came all this way just to see you."

"Yeah, I came all this way just for you," he said with a look of mirth in his eyes. Then that lock of hair fell over his eye and she just had to brush it aside.

How frustrating! Olivia felt like putting her mom back on the train and then tossing her off. Didn't she realize how much even one more minute in Alex's presence would hurt? How much it would devastate her, and him.

Everyone waited for her answer and Mari really needed to get back to the ship to recover, so Olivia decided to go ahead and get it over with. "Well, since you came so far, I guess we could do some hiking, I mean I wore my hiking boots." She wouldn't tell him that she'd already planned to take a hike that afternoon.

Chapter 7

Olivia started their hike being just a little bit annoyed at Alex for showing up unannounced, but now she was getting *really* annoyed. What made him think that he could just show up and she would drop everything to be with him? Well, at this particular time she would, but that wasn't the point, he was being mighty presumptuous concerning her feelings and she didn't like it.

They started out walking to a nearby trailhead and when Alex tried to grab her hand, she pulled it away.

"You don't like me touching you all of a sudden?" he asked. "You didn't seem to mind yesterday. Remember?"

Olivia felt her body flush and she was sure her face was red. Was she blushing or was she just angry at him. It was hard to tell at this point, because she felt like she should be both embarrassed and angry. "I just don't like you assuming that I want to be lovey dovey with you every time we see each other." What the hell was she saying? She was going to ruin their budding new friendship if she didn't back off, but damn it, she was upset.

Alex just smiled and grabbed her hand, pulling her farther along the trail. She couldn't bring herself to pull away this time, her anger just seemed to melt with his smile.

They walked for a while shrouded in silence, enjoying the scenery and the peace and quiet. Finally, Olivia decided there was something she just had to know. "How did you get here, Alex?

"I flew a plane."

"Your boss not only gave you time off to follow a woman, but they let you use one of the planes in which to do it?" she asked incredulously.

"Well yeah, he's a pretty generous guy."

"Sounds like he's insane to me," she mumbled. "Wait a minute, you said guy? So your aunt doesn't own the tour company anymore?"

"Not since my uncle died," he replied. He quickly pulled her behind a tree and kissed her. He had to change the subject so she wouldn't find out that he owned and ran the company successfully. That showed ambition, which she'd always said he didn't have. Could she accept him if she still thought he was a slacker? That was one thing he absolutely had to find out.

Olivia pulled away. “Don’t do that Alex.”

“Why not, you like it don’t you?”

“No, I don’t.”

“Yeah, okay,” he chuckled.

Alex pulled her back onto the main path and they walked along in a comfortable silence again for a while. He led her onto a second path, to the left, where the trees thinned a bit. He had only hiked this trail once, about a year ago, but he remembered it like it was moments ago. It would be the easiest one for Olivia and it wasn’t very crowded so they could be somewhat alone together. Maybe he could sneak a few more kisses.

Olivia spied a fallen log that she could sit on to re-tie her shoe, so she pulled away from Alex and walked over to it. She should have known better, sitting down was a big mistake. The shock of what happened to her sister was finally ready to really settle in. Her legs became shaky and she really didn’t know if she could stand up again.

Alex noticed that she had suddenly seemed to lose all of her fight, she even looked pale. Maybe if they took part in some general chitchat, it would keep her mind off of whatever was bothering her. "How did you like going through the tunnel on the train?" Alex asked as he stood nearby waiting for her to rest.

"Awesome," it came out as a cry.

Olivia was looking at the ground so he couldn't see her face, but he knew there was something really wrong. He walked over to her and sat down.

"What's wrong, Livia? Did I do or say something? If I did I'm really sorry."

She looked up at him and there were tears running down her face. She launched herself into his arms, nearly knocking him off the log.

"Whoa, what's wrong, Doll?"

Everything spilled out, along with many tears, she just couldn't help herself. Alex had always been one of her greatest confidants. The best, next to her twin.

Olivia told him about Mari's fall, and how her sister and Graham had almost lost each other. She told him that she might just hate her job, her friends, where she lived and how she lived. She told him that she thought she might still love him, but also how she just couldn't bring herself to give up the life she had worked so hard to build for herself – the life it seemed she might just hate.

He just held her and let her talk until no more words would come out. Then it was his turn to talk. "I understand Livia, I really do. I know what it's like to have a life you hate and not know what to do to make it better." He assured her. "I did that once, remember. You were the only thing in my life that was good, the only thing I didn't want to change."

On the train she'd realized how mean she'd been to him, but she never knew how much he'd hated his life. "You really were miserable weren't you?" she stated. "I'm so sorry I nagged you so much, I guess I just didn't realize how terrible you felt." She looked up at him. "I should have realized that we weren't right for each other sooner. We really should have ended it with a little more tact, you know."

"It's okay Olivia, it was partly my fault. I never really told you how I felt and I never let you know how much my heart broke every time you acted disappointed in me. I really thought we could work through things."

"I really hurt you didn't I?"

He just nodded and pulled her closer.

"I didn't mean to Alex, I really didn't." She took a deep steadying breath before saying the one thing she didn't want to say, but knew she had to. "You know, spending this time together is really a bad idea. We should just go our separate ways, I don't want to hurt you anymore than I already have."

Alex just held her and stroked her hair. He couldn't let her go. Not yet, maybe not ever. "You know, *I* think we should see each other every day that you have left here in Alaska and enjoy each other while we can. I know that for me, whether we go our separate ways now or in a few days, I'll hurt the same."

Olivia just sat there resting her head on his chest. She could hear his heart beating. "Yeah, you're right I guess, but how would we do that? The cruise is fully booked and I think my parents would object if I abandoned their family trip altogether," she asked.

"I can follow you to your ports of call in my…um, in the plane." Pearl's idea really was good!

"Are you really willing to follow me from port to port?" she asked, amazed at his offer. It warmed her heart that he would go to so much trouble and expense.

"Of course I am, in fact I would follow you almost anywhere right now."

"Except back home," she hedged.

"Yeah, I just can't do that, Doll. I'm so sorry. I just couldn't live like that again."

"I understand." She nodded. But what about your job, isn't it your busy season?" she asked.

"Like I said, the boss is a generous guy."

He lifted her chin with one finger and kissed her gently on the lips. She returned the kiss, and then deepened it. Picking her up, he slid her onto his lap. He needed to get as close as he possibly could.

Olivia groaned and mentally urged him to touch her burning skin. He must have heard, because his hand quickly slipped under her shirt and found her silk covered breast.

As Alex marveled at the feel of her he couldn't help but wonder what color her bra was this time. Bright and vibrant like the previous day, or dark and sexy like he preferred?

Running her hands underneath his shirt and up his back, she savored the heat and smoothness of his bare flesh. She wanted to rid him of all of his clothes right there in the middle of nowhere. But then she heard a snap from somewhere in the trees and she reluctantly pulled away.

"We can't do this here, there are other people around."

"Yeah, I guess you're right." He was trying hard to control his breathing.

"Do you have a hotel room?" she asked, "Maybe we could go there?"

"I already checked out. I have to fly away from here tonight." He smiled and kissed her forehead.

"Well, well look who we ran into son," they heard from behind Olivia. When she turned, her father and brother were standing on the trail.

"Hi guys, looks like we decided to hike the same trails." Olivia said, hoping her brother didn't notice her tear streaked face and freak out like he'd done on the train with Graham and Mari.

"Yep, we're going about another quarter of a mile in that direction," Ethan informed them, as he pointed the same way Olivia and Alex had been headed.

"I think we're going to head back and take the other trail," Alex said. "We just stopped to tie a shoe."

Jackson chuckled disbelievingly and started to walk on. "See you back on the ship sis, don't do anything I would."

"I'm not into Thomas little brother. You might have to fight Vanessa for him." She hollered after him, jokingly.

"Ha ha, very funny little brat!" Jackson, hollered back, stopping in his tracks. "Thomas isn't my type either, he prefers redheads with big boobies, my hair is brown and my boobies are flat, kind of like yours."

Olivia gaped at her brother and then laughed, the sound ringing through the trees. And soon Jackson and Ethan disappeared.

"I truthfully hope your brother doesn't really believe you have flat boobs," Alex said running his hand up under her shirt and caressing the overflowing handful of firm yet soft flesh he found there.

"Forget about my brother, let's just think of some place we can go to be together, Alex. Please."

He pulled her onto her feet and stood beside her. "Let's go, I know the perfect place. It's a bit of a climb, but I'll take you there if you want me to."

"God yes! Let's go," she cried.

They doubled back to where they took the path to the left and took the right one instead. Alex held her hand the whole way, helping her up and down the more difficult terrain. She was beginning to wonder what the hell she'd been thinking in taking this hike when they stepped up a slight incline and into a clearing. Before them was the most beautiful sight Olivia had ever seen. A waterfall jutted out of a cliff. It must have been twenty feet wide and thirty feet tall.

"I hope you don't mind getting wet," Alex warned. "The cliff is rounded so there isn't a space between the water and the cavern."

"After that hike, I'll welcome it!" Olivia answered. "Are you sure there is a cavern back there? It looks like a solid cliff."

Alex took her hand and pulled her toward the side of the waterfall. "Hold your breath and walk straight through, quickly."

She took a deep breath and they plunged through together. They were suddenly in a large cavern and the peace was amazing, surrounded in a rock cocoon. The only sound was of the running water and even that was muted.

"This is amazing!" Olivia exclaimed. "Thank you so much!"

"For what, Doll?"

"For finally getting me to appreciate and enjoy stuff like this," She smiled at him and then went back to exploring the cavern with her eyes.

"I'm glad I, and Alaska, were the ones to finally do it," he murmured as he pulled her close to kiss her.

"Are you cold?" he finally asked, wrapping his arms around her shivering body.

"No, just excited beyond belief." She whispered. "Are you sure no one will come back here?"

Alex laughed. "Most people don't even know there's a cavern."

Olivia nodded. "I'm not even going to ask how you know about it then," she said lightheartedly.

"I've never had a woman back here, Olivia. There hasn't been anyone since we broke up."

"I really wasn't worried," she exclaimed. "But I can't say the same. I kind of went looking for something I could never find after we broke up."

Alex smiled. "I'm not worried either Love, I'm glad you didn't hide away and stop living your life like I did for that first year."

She pulled him to her for another kiss and he ran his hands up under her shirt. She broke free and pulled the damp, clinging garment up over her head and dropped it to the ground. Alex followed her lead and stripped his dripping shirt from his muscled torso. She reached for the button on her jeans, but he moved to stop her.

"Let me."

She gasped when his work roughened hands grazed the delicate skin of her abdomen. She would never get tired of his touch.

Once the button and zipper were taken care of, he removed her shoes and socks, and slowly peeled the damp jeans from her body, inch by inch until she was wearing nothing but black silk and lace.

"Black this time! I was hoping," he sighed. "Black was always my favorite on you."

"I know, I was thinking of you when I picked them out this morning." She kissed him again as she made quick work of his button and zipper, but she made no move to rid him of the jeans. Her hand dipped inside his boxer briefs to free and tease him with her touch. She stroked him exactly the way she knew he liked best. For a brief moment, it felt like nothing had ever changed, no time had passed. It felt too good. "Doll please we're not going to get very far if you don't stop touching me like that."

"Touch *me* then."

Alex ran his right hand over her abdomen and down to the small piece of black silk and lace between her thighs. She shivered in anticipation as his left hand dipped inside her bra to gently squeeze her breast before running his thumb across her nipple.

His hands left her body for the briefest of moments to help her shimmy out of her panties and then they were back to where they'd left off. She broadened her stance to allow him better access and his finger slipped inside her.

"Oh Alex," she whispered. She wanted to say more but when his finger found the spot that spiked her pleasure, she lost all words. She grabbed him and kissed him instead.

His hands went to her hips and he backed up, pulling her with him until his thighs came up against a boulder. He sat and lifted Olivia to straddle his lap. She stroked him again, enjoying the familiarity of the look in his eyes. Holding him steady with one hand, she put her lips to his ear. "Now," she whispered as she lowered herself onto him in one piercing movement.

"Yes!" he hissed as he grabbed her hips to hold her still, savoring the first moments of pleasure. He pulled back and their eyes locked. His grip loosened.

She moved frantically, sliding up and driving down, grinding her hips against overwhelming pleasure. Three years of not seeing, tasting, touching or loving each other boiled over into that one moment when they lost complete control and came back down to earth together.

Olivia rested her forehead on Alex's shoulder. "Shit," she mumbled. She pulled away quickly and started to gather her clothes. She made sure to keep her back to Alex as she dressed.

"Livia, are you okay?" Alex sensed that something was wrong.

"I'm fine," she mumbled, but he heard the tears in her voice. He walked up behind her and wrapped his arms around her waist. "What's wrong, Love?"

She slumped forward, her upper body shaking.

He forced her to turn around and held her tight, stroking her back. "What's wrong? Talk to me, Doll."

"That was just too much for me Alex. I'm more confused than ever." She looked at him and took his face in her hands. "I love you but I can't be with you. I'm not sure what to do anymore."

He took her hands from his face and squeezed them. "There's no rush, Olivia. Take your time and think. If you do decide to be with me, it has to be because that's what you want more than anything else in this world."

She nodded her head. "I know Alex, and I think we should refrain from being intimate until I can figure some stuff out. The intensity of...of us, just confuses me more."

"Whatever you need sweetheart. I won't touch you until you say I can," he promised.

"Thank you, Alex."

He smiled and handed her the hiking boots he'd picked up from the ground. "You have to be starving?" It was more of a question than a statement.

"I am," she admitted as she put her boots on.

"Let's head back and I'll take you to lunch. I know the perfect place."

She stood up, grabbed his hand and they walked back through the waterfall together.

Their afternoon of lunch and exploring Skagway together went way too fast and before Olivia knew it, it was time to board the ship again. "I don't want to go yet," she admitted with tears in her eyes.

"I don't either, but I have to be getting on to Juneau and you have to get on the ship before it leaves you." He would give anything to pick her up, carry her to his plane and fly her home to Ketchikan, but he couldn't.

"I know, I just wish...where should I meet you tomorrow?"

"Right as you get off the ship, you'll see a tram. Meet me at their ticket booth okay," he said.

"Okay," she replied quietly.

He kissed her and started to walk away. Then he turned back. "Olivia?"

She turned to him with a smile on her face and tears in her eyes.

"Plan on 'missing' the ship tomorrow. I'll make sure you get to Sitka on time and I promise I won't touch you."

She nodded before turning around and walking toward the gangplank.

****

Olivia's curiosity was peaked and the excitement of the unknown was coursing through her. She couldn't imagine what he had planned. The thought of spending an entire night with him sent chills thorough her. They wouldn't be having sex, but they would still have almost twenty-four hours together to see how compatible they still were.

Olivia really didn't feel like getting ready for dinner, in fact, she didn't feel like going to dinner at all, but if she didn't show up, her mother would probably have a fit, and arguing with Charlotte was not an option. She would keep the peace for now so it would be easier to break the news that she wouldn't be there the following night. Of course the matchmaker would want to know why, but telling her why wasn't an option. Charlotte would gloat and assume that her plan was working.

Olivia finally decided to sit through dinner even if it meant ignoring her mother, and boy was she glad she did. Graham proposed to Mari. Technically they were still married, but he wanted to give her a real wedding and a real ring. It was all so romantic and it didn't hurt her to see them make things final. She just hoped this one success wouldn't make her mother ramp things up for the other couples who were being matched.

After the family dinner and a congratulatory hug to the happy couple, Olivia escaped to her room to plan for her big day in Juneau. The first thing she did was pack a bag with both warm and cold weather outfits, and the bare minimum of incidentals, and then she called it good.

Vanessa walked in when she was about done. "Where are you going?" she asked puzzled.

"Tomorrow when I leave the ship, I won't be coming back until Sitka."

"It must be great to have a personal pilot," she joked.

"Ah yes! It *is* fabulous. He does more than fly me places you know, he kisses me and hugs me, and..." She winked at her sister. She didn't bother telling Vanessa that she and Alex had an abstinence pact.

Vanessa laughed. It was so good seeing Olivia approaching something close to happiness again. "You know what? I want to know what is going on. As of this afternoon you didn't seem to want to see Alex again." She pulled Olivia onto the couch next to her. "Let me call Thomas and tell him to wait a few minutes and then you can tell me everything."

"No, you go to Thomas and I will tell you everything at breakfast," Olivia said. Her sister was obviously burning to see her new man.

Vanessa thought about it for a minute. "Okay, but only if you promise."

"I promise," Olivia said as she pulled her sister off the couch and pushed her toward the door.

With her bag packed and ready to go, she climbed into the shower, loving how the warm spray felt on her bare skin. Then suddenly she felt worn down. She cried

She cried for Mari because she had almost been seriously injured or killed, she cried for the heartbreak she might cause Alex and she cried for the heartbreak she might cause herself. And finally, she cried for all of the confusion she felt. If she cried today, she would be able to spend the next few days with Alex without worrying about whether the end would bring pain or not. Otherwise, their brief time together would be hampered by flashes of what may or may not happen.

Getting out of the shower, she dried herself off and dressed in a pair of shorts and a tank top. She felt a lot better and was able to get really excited about spending the night in Juneau again. She sat down on the end table to look out the window, feeling so at peace just watching the coastline pass by. Her body started to relax and her mind turned to thoughts other than Alex. Like telling her mother that she was going to miss a family dinner. Talk about spoiling a good time.

Reluctantly getting up from the nightstand, she sighed and sat down at the desk to call her mother and let her know what was going on. She wasn't even sure what she was going to say, but it had to be done. Before she could dial, there was a knock on the door, and she opened it to Jackson, who seemed to be in a much better mood than he had in a long time.

"Hey, can I come in Liv? I told Thomas and Vanessa that they could have some time alone."

"Yes, get in here. Now I don't have to call mother and try to be evasive with her," Olivia said, feeling relieved.

"Why would you need to be evasive with mother dear?" he asked curiously.

"Because I'll be leaving the ship tomorrow and I won't be back until Sitka. And of course, she'll think that it's because her plan is working. But then when she realizes that Alex and I are going to spend as much time together as we can during this vacation, but after that we will probably go back to our own lives, she will freak out, and then...who knows what. The point is, I'm dreading talking to her."

Jackson took his jacket off and made himself comfortable on the small couch. "How about I tell her for you, tomorrow, after you are safely in Juneau with Alex," he suggested.

"Would you?" she asked excitedly.

"Of course, it's the least I could do after what I put you through earlier in the week," He lamented. "Besides, what are twins for?"

"Thank you so much Jack. I owe you one."

All she had to drink was water or soda so she offered to order something up from room service, but Jackson wanted to stay away from alcohol until he knew his emotions were completely under control. He still had the monumental task of telling their mother and other siblings about his big secret. They settled for soda instead and continued to talk.

"So, I guess mom's plan will fail with you and Alex."

"Most likely. I do have doubts now and I've thought about it some, but our lives are just *so* different. I don't see it working out at all."

"You don't like your life, Livia. So why not try something new." He stated matter of fact.

"I have no idea what you are talking about Jackson. My life is just fine," she bit back. She hoped she sounded convincing, because her mind was replaying the scene from earlier where she admitted to Alex that she hated her life but couldn't imagine it being any other way.

"I don't believe you, Olivia. I know you hate your life. I live most of it with you, remember?"

She decided it was time to change the subject. Her brother did know her well, too well for comfort in this conversation.

"Do you want Michael to live with us until I sell you the townhouse and move out, or are you going to get a place of your own?" She figured this subject was much safer.

"I don't know for sure, but I have been thinking about buying a house, so he'll have a big yard. You won't be mad if I don't buy the townhouse from you, will you?"

"Of course not! It's a good place, it'll sell quickly. Besides, I was kind of thinking of keeping it and staying put for a while. Save up some more money before buying the house I want."

Olivia was both sad and excited to see the progression in her twin's life. He had possibly found his true love again and gained a son in such a short amount of time. He must be reeling. She really couldn't wait to see him with his son though, he was going to be such a good dad. But she was also sad that his life seemed to be taking a new path, far away from hers.

They talked a lot more about Michael and what Jackson wanted to do for him. She was surprised to find out that he had been talking to the little boy via the internet every day for over a week. The tone of his voice and the look in his eyes told her he was a proud dad already and loved Michael very much. It made her feel even better – her brother would never be alone again. She on the other hand had a very good chance of being alone for a long time to come.

Vanessa and Thomas had about three hours alone and Olivia was getting tired so Jackson decided to go back to his own cabin, or maybe out to the bar. He couldn't help but say one final thing on the subject of Alex before he left though. "It breaks my heart that I didn't get the chance to fight for my one true love, sis. It also breaks my heart that you refuse to fight for yours because you're scared and have a warped sense of what life needs to be like. Wake up Liv, and fight for him before it's too late." He kissed her on the forehead and was gone.

What Jackson said was meant to be a big revelation for her, but their previous conversation about her townhouse and about wanting to see him as a dad had brought back some of her resolve to keep with her current lifestyle. She had a life she was proud of! Didn't she?

Her twin's advice did have merit though. What if she really did hate her life and she lost Alex again? Could she ever find true happiness? Would she want to? Her resolve started to wane again.

Great! She suddenly felt like crying. It seemed she was getting more and more confused with each hour that passed. Another shower was out of the question, so crawling under the covers would have to do.

Just as she was dozing off her phone rang. She saw Alex's name come across the caller ID. "Hello Alex."

"Hello Olivia, how are you? You don't sound so good."

"I'm not sure," she answered. "I'm still so confused and sad, and it seems like my family and my overworked mind are just making it worse."

"I'm sorry Doll, I wish I could help, but I won't push you in either direction. Just know that I'm here for you, always."

"Thank you, Alex."

"I'm going to let you get some sleep. I'll see you tomorrow morning. Okay?"

"Okay, Alex. I miss you."

"I miss you too."

Olivia hung up the phone and sat up in bed waiting for the text she knew would come. Five minutes later it did. It said, *I still love you*, and she was able to lie back down and cry herself to sleep.

Chapter 8

Olivia's second cry did her a world of good, she woke up feeling refreshed and ready to start the day. She would be seeing Alex in just over an hour and she wouldn't leave his side for almost twenty-four hours. She couldn't wait!

While she dressed, she contemplated not telling Vanessa everything, just in case her sister imparted unsolicited advice on her like Jackson had. Today must be perfect, no regrets and no sadness allowed.

Finally deciding that she couldn't go back on her promise, Olivia told Vanessa everything that was going on with Alex as they ate breakfast at the Café Wave Buffet. Her sister listened closely and seemed to be really interested in what was being said, but Olivia could sense that some advice would be coming, so she braced herself.

"So, let me get this straight, you love Alex, the reasons why you had trouble being with him are fading, and you actually like Ketchikan, but you still won't get off your butt and go be with the man you love?"

"That sounds kind of harsh, Nessa! You just don't understand." Olivia exclaimed. "My life is good and I've worked *so* hard for everything I have."

"You've worked hard for everything but Alex, for everything but love." Vanessa reminded her.

Olivia flinched.

"And you don't love your life, what you do, or who you've become!" Vanessa stated. "It's time for a change big sister."

"Sheesh, have you been talking to Jackson or something?" Olivia asked. "How in the hell would you know that I'm not happy?"

"It's obvious, Livia. It's been obvious for a long, long time, probably even back when you and Alex were still together."

Olivia scoffed at her baby sister. There is no way anyone could know she was unhappy before she did. It just wasn't possible. Was it?

"From what you've told me, I think you *will* give up your silly 'my precious, perfect life' scenario and be with the man you love. When it'll happen, I don't know, but it *will* be soon," Vanessa proclaimed, almost daring her sister to argue again.

So much for a completely perfect day. "What, are you psychic now?" Olivia retorted. Every ounce of frustration she felt toward her sister came pouring out in her voice. It should be her decision if she wanted to change her life, not everyone else's! She would be the first to know. Wouldn't she? Of course she would, the thought that someone else would know what she was feeling better than she did was ridiculous.

"Just you wait and see," was all Vanessa had to say after that, and the rest of the meal was taken in silence.

Before Olivia knew it, it was time to leave the ship to meet Alex at the tram office. She was so excited she found herself running to the exit. All of the conversations with her siblings from the past two days were pushed aside and Alex was what she concentrated on now.

****

Was there a city in Alaska that Olivia wouldn't like? Juneau was absolutely beautiful and of course it was drizzling so she was even happier. There was something about the rain that made everything feel so fresh and new.

She half walked, half ran to the tram office which wasn't far from the ship, and she searched for Alex among the people milling around. She didn't see him at all. Where was he? Hopefully he would be there soon, she was getting more and more anxious to see him.

"Hi beautiful," she heard coming from behind her. She turned and Alex was leaning against the railing with one leg crossed over the other, looking completely sexy in faded jeans, a black t-shirt, and his hiking boots. She almost forgot to breathe, and then when that one lock of his perfectly groomed hair fell over his eye, she thought for sure her heart would stop beating. She was so happy to see him again.

He picked up the black hoodie, laying on the rail next to him, and walked over to her. She threw her arms around his neck and kissed him, and when they pulled apart, she noticed that only one of his arms was holding her, the other was tucked behind his back.

"What are you hiding," she asked

"Just this." He smiled and brought his hand around to present her with a single pink rose.

"Oh my God! You didn't forget?"

"Of course I didn't, I'll never forget anything about you, Olivia Rachelle Mannon."

"Oh Alex, I just don't know what to say."

"Don't say anything, Love." He kissed her gently and pulled away to look into her eyes. "You said you were sad last night so I brought you a pink rose. It's what I promised to do right?"

She chuckled. "Yeah, it's just that you made that promise so long ago..."

"A promise is a promise, Olivia." He kissed her again. And when they pulled apart, he slipped into his hoodie and they walked up the ramp to the tram boarding area.

"First, I thought we could go see Mount Roberts and then we will decide where to go from there. Maybe I could take you someplace extra special."

"Whatever you want to do, this is your turf," she answered. "I'm up for anything."

"I'll remember that, Living Doll," he said winking at her.

Did he want to forget their no sex deal? She did, but she knew she wouldn't, at least she would try her hardest not to. She would just have to remind herself of all of the good reasons not to sleep with him again...yet.

Alex spent the tram ride with his arms wound tightly around Olivia, enjoying the feel of her, the smell of her – just being so near her. "Is this kind of touching okay?" he whispered.

"Absolutely," she answered.

The trees, the mountain, and the fog wrapped slowly, snugly around them as they climbed higher and higher. Pretty soon it was like they were in another world. Olivia was not prepared for the beauty that confronted her when she stepped off the tram.

"Oh Alex, I have never seen anything like this in my life."

"That's why I brought you here. I wanted you to see this place. To see how beautiful the world can be."

"Thank you," she whispered and stood on her tiptoes to kiss him.

They skipped the gift shops and headed straight for the hiking trails. Alex pointed things out that just days ago she would never have thought to look for; squirrels and other assorted small creatures, trees of all kinds, wildflowers and bushes in random places and birds flying free. The eagles were just breathtaking, they were what fascinated Olivia the most. How could one small creature be so majestic, so beautiful?

Alex noticed the look of awe on her face as she watched the birds of prey leave the trees. "The feeling that you get when you look at one of them take flight is the same feeling I get when I take up one of the planes. It's fear, freedom and exhilaration all rolled into one." He really needed to make her see how happy flying, and therefore his new life, made him.

"I never thought of it like that," she replied with tears of joy in her eyes. "No wonder you love it so much."

"I do love it. There is nothing I would rather do than take to the skies. Well maybe except for making love to you, forever." He stopped and moved away from her. "I'm so sorry, Livia. I never should have said that."

"It's okay Alex, I never said we couldn't talk about sex." In all actuality, she wished they could do more than talk.

Instead they walked farther along the path and Olivia knew what true happiness felt like for the first time in a long time. Maybe her brother and sister were right. "I used to think life made me feel happy like you feel now, but I'm not so sure anymore."

"Give it time," he whispered as he gathered her into his arms. "Everything will become clear to you in time. You'll know exactly what makes you happy, what makes you complete. It might be a career, or a hobby, or just a place you like to be. It could be more than one thing." Alex told her. "You will feel it deep down in your soul and there will be no mistaking it. "I know Doll, it's finally started to happen to me. There's only one piece missing."

Olivia rested her cheek on his chest. She wanted to believe him, but it was hard.

She was twenty-four years old, so how long would it take to find the things that made her feel complete, she felt like time was running out. She was still so young though, so why did she feel like that so often. And if it was true, that she would just know it when it happened, then it obviously hadn't happened yet. It hurt too much to admit that maybe she'd been fooling herself all along. Her world wasn't as complete, or perfect as she'd always thought it was.

They walked together in silence for quite a while. Olivia was thrilled when she noticed birds she had only seen in books or magazines. In the city, it was common to see only pigeons and crows. She stopped every once in a while just to watch the small winged creatures at play, or watch them take to the sky to find their special place in the world. "You know Alex," she said, breaking the silence. "For the first time in my life, I feel like I can really breathe." She demonstrated by taking a deep breath of fresh, cool air.

Alex loved watching her discover all of these new things. It was like watching a kid at Christmas. "I never noticed while I lived in Vegas or Seattle, but once I moved here I discovered the same thing." Wrapping his left arm around her shoulder, he guided her back onto the path. "You know, my dad used to say that big cities and extreme heat clogged your lungs, your pores and your soul so that you practically stopped breathing. He believed that a person had to have fresh, cool air, at least occasionally, to survive."

"I like that, I think he was right. Olivia suddenly felt sad. "You said your dad *used* to say it, what's going on?"

Alex stopped walking and looked to the sky. "My parents are gone, Livia. They, and my Uncle, died two years ago." He took a deep, shaky breath. "They were sailing when a big storm hit. You know, Pearl would have been gone too if she hadn't stayed home sick that day."

Olivia saw tears in his eyes. "Oh God, Alex! I'm so sorry. I loved your parents and I missed them so much after we broke up."

"They missed you too, and they never passed up an opportunity to let me know how much they missed you," he stated.

Olivia saw a smile through the tears shining in his eyes. "You came here when they died?"

"Yeah, I needed someone to lean on and Pearl needed someone to help her out, so I moved here. It was the best decision I ever made, Living Doll. It's when I found what made me mostly complete – flying for a living, not just for fun, and Alaska. There was only one thing missing."

Olivia nodded at him and started walking again. This conversation would haunt her for a long time. It was such a shock to find out that his parents were gone. At one time, she had hoped they would become her in-laws. Her heart broke just thinking about what Pearl and Alex must have gone through.

She was lost in her own thoughts when Alex broke through with excitement in his voice. "Hey Livia, try this," he said, handing her a berry off of a nearby bush.

"Are you sure it's safe? They always warned us in school about eating strange things off of strange bushes," she said warily.

"I'm absolutely positive. Pearl has these growing in her back yard and they are the best tasting thing ever. I promise!"

She took the berry that he offered and put it into her mouth a bit hesitantly. "Oh wow! This is great."

"I told you so," He smiled at her as she enjoyed the tasty little berry. "Now this little snack has served to remind me that I'm very hungry. Would you like to go get something to eat?"

"Yes, I'm starving! Where should we eat?"

"It's a surprise. Now come on so we don't miss the next tram down the mountain."

They raced each other back to the platform and were out of breath when they reached the spot where they'd started their hike. Olivia turned around to take one last look at the beautiful place she was falling in love with. She felt so free, so peaceful there.

She really didn't want to go. How would it feel if she never saw this beautiful place again? And what she was thinking must have shown on her face because Alex pulled her into a hug. "If you love something that much, you'll find a way to get back to it." She briefly wondered if he was talking about Mt. Roberts or himself.

****

Alex drove his rental car for five minutes before he pulled into a busy parking lot.

"We're having lunch in a grocery store?" Olivia asked skeptically when she saw where they were.

Alex laughed. "No, I'm going to pick something up. Now wait here and I'll be right back." He came out, just a few minutes later, with a fully stocked picnic basket.

"Now that's what I call a great lunch," Olivia said as he put the basket in the back seat.

"I was hoping you'd like it. I know this great park where we can go and have a picnic. Are you up for it?"

"Yeah, let's go, the sun is shining now. It's the perfect day for this."

They didn't drive for very long before they pulled into a beautiful park with a ton of trees. When they were settled on a thick blanket at the edge of the grassy area, Alex set all kinds of food out in front of Olivia. Meats, cheeses and salads.

"What kind of cheese is this, Alex? It doesn't look familiar." She picked up a piece and tasted it.

Alex started laughing.

"What's so funny?"

"I have no idea what kind it is. I called the store this morning and asked them if they could put together a picnic basket for me and the sexiest, most beautiful woman in the world. I told them to put in whatever they thought was best."

Olivia started laughing too. The sound rang through the trees surrounding the park and Alex cherished every note. He'd missed hearing her laugh so much, and just having a calm, everyday conversation with her.

Rain started to pour down halfway through their meal. Alex grabbed the blanket and tossed it, food and all, into the picnic basket and they ran for cover inside the rental car. "Wow, I'm used to the rain, but that was quite a downpour," Alex said, chuckling.

"Yeah, it was cold too!" Olivia agreed.

He grabbed a red and black flannel shirt out of the back seat and ran it over his hair before handing it to her. "Dry your hair now," he offered. "It'll warm you up some." When they were both sufficiently dry and warm again, Olivia decided to see if she could salvage anything from their lunch. She only managed to save some cheese and crackers and a couple of mints, the rest was all mashed together, and Alex looked disappointed.

"I'd say this was the best meal I've ever had," she enthused.

"I was hoping you'd feel that way." He relaxed a bit and smiled at her. "I was thinking the same thing." He wondered when Olivia had started to enjoy something as simple as a rained out picnic.

The picnic basket was tossed into the back seat and he pulled Olivia close. He started to kiss her neck and nibble his way up to her ear, concentrating his efforts there for a moment. She shivered beneath his touch and he pulled away. "Are you cold?"

"No." She pulled him to her for a kiss. Her body shivered again as his hand traveled under her shirt and ultimately inside her lacy bra.

"I'd say you're quite warm," he whispered, relishing the heat emanating from her body.

"Keep doing that and I'll be downright hot," she murmured. She responded in kind when he deepened the kiss. God she wanted him so badly, right then, right there. Somewhere in the back of her mind, a voice whispered, "no sex."

"Okay, we need to stop Alex," she said, pulling away. "We said we weren't going to do this."

"I know, I'm sorry," he mumbled, running his fingers through his hair trying to regain control. "I have a late checkout at the hotel and I guess it's time to do that. We can grab my stuff and get on with the best part of our day together. You don't need to go to the ship do you?"

"No, everything I need is in my backpack." She buckled her seatbelt. "You said the best part is coming up, do I get any hints?"

Alex turned his famous grin on her and she had her answer. The rest of the day would be a complete surprise.

At the hotel, Olivia knew better than to go into his room with him because they would probably never make it out, and she had come too far to give up now. She waited for him in the lobby. Imagining what Alex had in store for her made her excited and nervous all at the same time. She couldn't fathom where he would take her, or what they would do when they got there. Knowing Alex, it was probably somewhere secluded and surrounded by nature. But for some reason, she didn't really mind. All that mattered was that she had Alex all to herself. There would be no one else around to meddle or interfere.

"Are you ready?" she heard from behind her.

Turning around, she smiled at Alex, hoping it conveyed her excitement. She was more than ready for anything he could dish out.

They drove for what seemed like forever to a small private air strip that Alex said his friend John owned.

"That's the plane we took the tour in isn't it, Alex?" she asked, pointing to the small plane sitting on the lake nearby.

"Yeah, that's my plane actually. She's a beauty isn't she?"

"She's great!" Olivia agreed. "You have your very own plane?"

Crap, he'd almost let the cat out of the bag. "Yeah, it was part of my inheritance."

Olivia nodded, what a great memory of his uncle. "We're flying somewhere today?"

"Yeah, but not in my plane. We'll take one of John's helicopters. That won't be a problem will it?"

"I hope not!" she exclaimed. I've never been on one, but I'm sure it'll be fine."

"You are in for the ride of your life!" he exclaimed as he grabbed her hand and led her into a little white building. They were in what could have passed for an aircraft museum. Memorabilia practically overran the small front room. Olivia liked it immediately.

"Hey Johnny," Alex called out.

A man of about fifty five or sixty appeared in the doorway to the back room. He was a giant of a man with long hair and a long beard. He wore torn jeans and tie-dye. She immediately felt comfortable with him, even if he did remind her of one of her stuck in the sixties college professors.

"Well, well Alex, so we finally get to meet Olivia." He walked over to her and took her hand in his. "She is a pretty little thing isn't she?"

"You sound like Pearl," Alex lamented.

"How is the old bat?" John asked.

"Same as always," Alex answered.

"Alexander Paige Junior, you get your butt over here right now." The sweet sing song voice came from behind John, but Olivia couldn't see anybody. And then a tiny woman stepped out from behind him, she had dark skin and deep brown eyes. And her dark hair hung down to her knees, she was absolutely the most beautiful woman Olivia had ever seen.

Alex walked over to her and picked her up in a big hug. He set her down right in front of Olivia. "Doll, this is Sue, she and this old man here are happily married. They were my parent's best friends."

"Damn straight we are, going on twenty-five years now." Sue pulled Olivia into a hug and whispered, "It's about time he brought you by. He's only been talking about you since the day he met you."

Olivia just smiled, Alex must have known them for most of his life. She'd had the feeling that he hadn't really talked about her to anyone, but she must have been wrong. They obviously knew a lot about her.

Let her go Sue, these two have to be leaving. I'm lending them one of the choppers for their trip," John said.

As they stepped outside, Sue called out to them. "Alexander! You bring her over to the house for a proper visit soon. You hear me." Alex just waved his hand as he walked away. Olivia didn't bother to tell Sue that she probably would never be back. Somehow, she didn't think the older woman would believe her.

John took them to the helicopter and bid them farewell and good luck. When they were safe inside the bird, Olivia started to get a bit nervous about her first helicopter ride. She knew it was going to be a completely different experience than an airplane. "Are you sure you can fly this thing Alex?" she asked skeptically.

He laughed at her. "Yes Olivia, I'm a licensed helicopter pilot. In another year, I...um I think Page Air Tours is planning on buying one of these magnificent machines." He had to remind himself that he didn't want her to know just yet that he actually owned the tour company, and he'd already slipped up earlier.. He was pretty sure now that she loved him no matter what, but he still wanted to be a hundred percent sure. He hoped this camping trip would be the push she needed and then he could tell her about his inheritance and how successful he'd made Paige Air Tours over the last two years.

Olivia lost her breath when they took off, it was one of the most magnificent feelings she'd ever experienced.

"It's great isn't it?" he asked her.

"That's an understatement," she answered breathlessly.

Alex concentrated on flying as Olivia took in the wonders surrounding her. Trees, rivers, meadows and wild animals lived in harmony below her. She had the best view in the world.

They were only in the air for half an hour and when Alex set the helicopter down in a beautiful meadow. Olivia didn't know for sure, but she had a feeling there was a river or stream gurgling somewhere nearby.

"What is this place? Where are we?"

"This is three hundred acres of the most beautiful land God made." Alex said with a sense of awe filling his voice.

"It's okay we're here though, right?" she asked.

"Yes sweetheart, we aren't going to get arrested for being here. John owns this land. He wants to make a sort of naturalist camp ground, preserving the wilderness, but still allowing people to experience the peace and beauty that's found here."

"Wow that would be quite an endeavor. He should be proud though, it's such a beautiful place.

"It is! Now you go sit down somewhere and enjoy this beautiful view while I pitch us a tent."

Olivia sat down in the soft grasses, but then she started to wonder about the tent. Were they going to spend the night here? In the wilderness. With wild animals all around. The biggest question though was could she handle that?

She'd been camping many times with her family, but she had always stayed in the camper or a cabin, safe, sound and warm. She should really talk to Alex about this. He knew she wasn't an outdoor camping kind of woman, especially with bears and the like around. She thought for sure he would have taken her to a cabin or someplace safe, yet still surrounded by the beautiful scenery.

"Alex, can I ask you a question?"

"What is it, Love?" he asked distractedly as he worked on the tent.

"Are we going to be here all night, with wild animals?" she hedged.

"Yes, we're going to spend the night, or most of it, together here. I want you to see how wonderful it can be, and how safe you are with me."

His last statement made her think and then it suddenly hit her. She was being set up. Alex was probably hoping that she would enjoy herself so much here that she would forget all about her city life and stay with him. Oh how infuriating. She didn't appreciate being tricked. It was the one way to make her not do something that was wanted of her.

Well, was he ever in for a shock. She was now determined to not like it there. Maybe she would even do a few things to make *him* not like it there. She decided to start by offering to help with the tent. That should be a disaster.

"Hey Alex, can I help you with the tent?" she said picking up one of the long poles laying nearby. She heard a squeak and then a groan and when she turned, Alex was on his knees holding his nether regions.

"Oh my God. Alex are you okay," she yelled dropping the pole and going to him. "What happened?"

"You…that pole…hit me." He moaned.

Okay, she wanted to make him not want her to be here, but she didn't want to injure him. "I'm so sorry Alex, I didn't mean to…" He held up his hand to stop her from talking more. He just wanted some quiet so he could catch his breath and get back to his feet.

When he finally stood, Olivia started fluttering around him. "Are you okay, can I get you something? Let me help!"

"I'm fine now, Livia. Just go sit down and let me finish the tent. And then maybe you can kiss it better."

Olivia felt a blush creep up her cheeks. What in the hell was wrong with her, she hadn't blushed so much in front of Alex since they'd first kissed.

"Are you sure I can't help you with the tent, Alex?" she asked more as a way to get her mind off of what she'd done than to actually offer help.

"No!" he hollered. And then quieter he said, "I have a feeling that if you helped me anymore, I would be in the hospital rather than here with you tonight."

Olivia felt her face warm again and went to sit down. She really was happy that he wasn't seriously injured. She was also pretty sure that the little accident with the tent pole would be a mark in the negative column for this trip. Olivia- one, Alex – zero.

"It's okay Doll, I know this isn't your kind of thing so I don't expect you to help. Maybe someday you'll learn and we can do it together, but for now, it's okay if you just take it easy and enjoy the scenery."

Okay so maybe this wasn't a negative for him. Damn it, why did he have to be so patient and understanding? And why was he assuming they would do this again?

When the tent was finally up, Alex came to sit by her. "We should probably gather some firewood soon and get a fire started. You could probably help me with that if you promise not to wield any sticks at my crotch."

She didn't laugh or answer him, she just kissed him. Sweet and slow. No matter how miserable she wanted to make this trip for him, she couldn't resist him. When she felt the need to kiss him, she just *had* to kiss him.

He pulled her down to lay next to him in the grass, his fingers playing a tune on her arm. He would take this over gathering firewood any day. "I'm sorry about what I said about kissing me better earlier. I kind of forgot about not being intimate."

"It's okay Alex, you were just joking around."

"Thank you, Olivia."

"For what," she asked.

"For coming here with me. I can't tell you how long I've wanted to show you this part of my life." He pulled her close and kissed her.

Now she felt guilty, Alex hadn't been trying to trick her, he'd truly wanted to show her something that was important to him.

"We should probably gather some firewood if we want to be warm and have dinner tonight."

Olivia reluctantly agreed. They needed to do something, or she would break their no sex pact.

Gathering firewood went without incident. Olivia worked hard and didn't complain, and they soon had a roaring campfire. She warmed her hands while Alex went to the helicopter to get their things.

"Two backpacks and a cooler, can I get you anything else my dear?" he asked as he put their stuff down near her.

"Um…yeah, how about a bathroom?"

"See that stand of trees over there?" Alex asked. Olivia slowly nodded. "Pick one and squat behind it."

Looking horrified, Olivia didn't quite know what to say. She was very close to demanding that he fly her back to John's and then take her to a nice hotel. But she just couldn't do that. A few days ago, she would have asked to go back, so why not now? The answer slowly came to her. If they left now, it would have to be his idea because she was done with being a spoiled brat who refused to try new things, at least outwardly.

"Here take this, everything you might need is in there. And when you are done, walk to the other side of the meadow and get us a bucket of water from the creek, please."

She stood and let out a disgusted sigh. She grabbed the pack and the collapsible bucket he held and headed for the trees. She just hoped she would actually be able to use these primitive outdoor facilities. If not, they would be in big trouble because she couldn't hold it all night.

As she walked away, she heard Alex chuckling. Boy would she show him. She wasn't quite sure how, but he would get his in the end, not for bringing her here which had been her original plan, but for laughing at her discomfort.

Alex was preparing for dinner when he heard Olivia scream. He was thinking she had probably seen something small and furry, so he just looked toward the trees expecting her to come running. Then he heard a splash coming from the opposite direction. Shit, she must have fallen into the creek. He took off running and when he arrived at the creek bed, Olivia rose out of the shallow water, soaked from head to toe, looking very angry. Uh oh, he was in for a tongue lashing now.

But it never happened. Olivia started to shiver so he ran to the tent to get one of their blankets and brought it back to her. “Take your clothes off sweetheart,” he ordered.

“No sex Alex, besides, I’m definitely not in the mood right now,” she returned.

“I mean, you’re wet and cold, take your clothes off and wrap yourself in this blanket.”

“Oh,” She blushed again.

When she was wrapped up and started to get warm, Alex gathered her clothes and helped her back to the campfire. Sitting her on the log he’d placed near the fire, he went to hang her clothes so they could dry, then he came back to check on the food.

“The beans are cooking nicely, why don’t you grab one of those hot dogs and put it on this stick.”

“Beans and wieners huh?”

“It wouldn’t be your first real campout without them,” he answered.

“I’ve been camping before,” she said stubbornly.

“An RV doesn’t count, Living Doll.”

She just shrugged. She had to admit that this particular campout was very different from the ones with her parents. Sure they’d had a fire and beans and wieners, but there sure were no tents and no sleeping bags. They really never roughed it.

"Here, hold this hot dog over the fire and I'll be right back," he said.

"Why, where are you going," she asked with just a hint of fear in her voice. He wasn't going to leave her there alone was he? It would probably be dark soon and then all sorts of creatures would come out.

"I'm going to the bathroom. Just stay here by the fire and you'll be fine. And just remember that it doesn't really get dark here this time of year."

God how did he always seem to know what she was thinking! "Okay." She held the hot dog over the fire and she realized that now was the time to do something else to make him regret laughing at her camping incompetence. How would he feel if she burned his dinner? A hungry man would not be a happy man. She stuck the hot dog deep into the fire and didn't pull it out until there were black strips down the sides of the stupid thing.

"Hey, how did you know how I like mine cooked?"

She turned to look at him. "You like them burned?" She was shocked.

"Yep, just like you got it. Burned ever so slightly, it's delicious, you should try it.

Olivia couldn't believe it. When would she ever learn? She could run a restaurant without making it crumble to the ground but she couldn't make a simple plan, to trick her boyfriend, succeed. Her ex-boyfriend. She'd said ex-boyfriend right?

She was smart enough to know when she'd been beat so she reluctantly decided to work on a new motto. If you can't beat 'em, join 'em. Yeah that was a good new motto to follow. Despite almost crippling Alex, peeing in the woods, and falling in the creek, she really was having a great time. In fact, she was beginning to wish she could spend more time like this with him. There was something intoxicating about the combination of fresh air, nature and Alex.

She didn't want to waste time making him miserable, she wanted to enjoy every minute with him. The problem was, the line between every minute for the next couple of days and for the rest of her life, was starting to blur. A lot. She didn't want to contemplate that though.

Olivia didn't realize how hungry she was until she ate two hot dogs and two helpings of beans. It was probably the best tasting meal she had eaten in a long time. And that was saying a lot considering their cruise ship was known to have some of the best food in the industry.

"Dessert?" Alex asked, pulling a bag of marshmallows out of the cooler.

"Now this is one thing I'm an expert at," she said happily as she stuck a marshmallow on the end of her stick. She felt like a kid again, like when her family had roasted marshmallows at Crater Lake, The Valley of Fire, or even in the back yard barbeque pit. This was the best dessert ever.

Alex and Olivia went through about half of the bag before they declared themselves full enough to burst. Now they were sticky and in need of some water to clean up with.

"Why don't you get inside the tent and I'll go get some water," Alex suggested, grabbing the collapsible pail from beside the fire. As soon as she'd had her fill of the beautiful fire, she planned to do just that.

"In a minute, I just want to enjoy the fire for a bit."

"Okay I'll be back in about ten minutes." He kissed her cheek.

Once Olivia finally stepped into the tent, she realized how warm it actually was inside their little haven. She slipped the blanket off her shoulders and let it fall to the floor. She heard Alex dousing the fire and hurried to sit on their makeshift bed.

When he walked in a few minutes later, his mouth dropped open and he almost dropped the pail of water all over their blankets.

Oh yeah, just the reaction she wanted!

"You know Alex, I don't know if I'll be able to sleep tonight without a bath," she said, leaning back on her elbows and rubbing her hand up and down her flat stomach, then letting it rest for a moment on the small red scrap of lace between her legs.

"But um..." He shook his head to clear his mind. "Didn't you sort of um...get clean earlier when you fell in the creek?"

"That blanket I was wrapped in made me so sweaty. Right here," she claimed, running her hand through the valley between her breasts. "And right here," she said, brushing one finger along the underside of each luscious breast. "I feel so dirty, Alex," She whispered.

For once, he was speechless, he just watched her and his body reacted to the sight and to the words she uttered so seductively. Finally after quite an effort, he managed to speak. "The water's cold sweetheart, are you sure you want to wash your entire body with it?"

"I want *you* to wash my entire body, Alex. Besides, the colder the better, then you can turn around and make me hot all over again."

"Ah shit!" he walked to his pack and took out a clean cloth. Then he knelt beside her and started to wash her hands. When they were no longer sticky, he moved his attention to her neck and chest. Her breathing quickened as the cold cloth came in contact with the sensitive skin above her breasts. The water was freezing, but her body was so hot with her desire for Alex that there should have been steam wafting off of her.

Kissing all of the areas he'd just been over with the cloth, Alex could feel Olivia quivering beneath him. His excitement spiked just knowing what he did to her.

He dipped the cloth back into the water and wrung it out. He flattened it and placed it over one gorgeous breast. When he lifted it, her nipple was puckered and begging for attention.

She arched her back at the feeling of his warm tongue on her nipple and he had to still her by grabbing hold of her waist. He let his hands rest there as he gave her other breast the same treatment.

As the cloth made its way down her stomach and hips, she didn't know how much more she could take. When she felt the cool creek water drip onto her most intimate part, she gasped and lifted her hips to the sensation. And then a whole new feeling took over when she felt the warmth of his hands and then his mouth. She sighed and settled back down to enjoy the pleasure of his tongue working the treasure he'd found. He took his time at this course of play and her body began to pulse, she was close to falling into the dark, but before she started her descent, the sensation was gone. Alex had pulled away again. Olivia almost felt like crying, except she knew that whatever was to come next would be even better.

Alex undressed and sat back down next to her. "Turn over, Livia," he whispered in her ear right after he kissed her desire swollen lips.

Cold creek water dripped on her back as Alex washed down her spine and across her butt and then down her legs. He repeated the trail in reverse with his lips and when he reached the small of her back, she felt him nudging her legs apart and instinctively, she lifted her hips to allow him access to whatever he may want. He moved over her and slowly, painstakingly slid inside her and the pleasure was so intense he had to stop for a moment to gather his senses before moving again, he could barely handle the heat.

"Alex, please. Please bring me home," she whispered. And he knew she was not only talking about her climax, but also her feelings about their future together. It wouldn't be long now until they were together for good. He just had to be patient.

Physically though, his patience was gone and he moved hard against her, burying himself as deep as he could go, again and again. His heart beat pounded with the same rhythm as their bodies, and he brought her crashing home. Then he came home too.

He rolled her onto her back and they lay holding each other not daring to speak of the pact they'd so blatantly broken.

Just before Alex fell asleep, he heard Olivia whisper, "I love everything about you Alexander Timothy Paige Jr., I always have." He just hoped that when the passion cleared from their minds in the morning, she would remember that she felt that way.

Chapter 9

Olivia woke trying to remember where she was and then her eyes settled on the most magnificent sight. Alex was standing in front of the open tent with his back to her, the beautiful landscape spread out before him. He was completely naked.

God she loved him. Now that she was finally admitting it, one hundred percent to herself, what would she do about it? She remembered whispering the words to him the night before, but she was pretty sure he hadn't heard. She wasn't quite ready for him to hear it yet. If things turned sour, it would only hurt him more to know how she felt.

They only had two more days of being in the same state; all day in Sitka, then she would be alone on the ship for a day, and then they might have a few hours in Seward or Anchorage before she flew home and he flew back to Ketchikan. She wasn't ready for this to end yet. How could she have been so wrong about her two crying episodes on the ship? They were meant to get all of her emotions out but they obviously hadn't. Here she was, a full thirty-six hours early, feeling like her world was about to end in a fiery crash of pain and emotion. Tears sprang to her eyes and she sat up quickly, trying to get the thoughts out of her head. She couldn't let this bother her, not yet.

"It's still early Love, go back to sleep for a bit," Alex whispered, without even turning around.

"Alex!" His name came out as an anguished cry.

He rushed to her side and held her close. "I was standing there thinking about how much I don't want all of this to end," he confided, lifting her chin so she would look at him. "Is that what you're thinking about too?"

She nodded and let her head fall to his shoulder. He could feel her tears as she shook in his arms.

"Don't cry Livia, you're breaking my heart."

"I can't help it," she mumbled. "I'm so damn confused and no matter what I do or think, I just get more confused."

"I'm sorry Love, I guess we shouldn't have gone back on our pact last night."

"It's not that Alex, I'm fine with what we did. We both have to return to our lives soon and we needed that, hell maybe it will have to last me for the rest of my life…"

"Olivia, please look at me."

She pulled away and dried the tears from her eyes.

"I love you, and more than anything in this world I want you to come to Ketchikan to be with me. Forever. But if that isn't going to happen, I just want you to know that this has been the absolute best week of my life. Last night will by no means last me a lifetime, but I will never forget one minute of anything we had this time around." Alex sighed and stroked the side of her face. "I hope it will be the same for you."

Olivia smiled at him. "I won't forget anything either Alex, I promise."

He kissed her and found himself having trouble letting go.

"Please make love to me one last time," she whispered desperately

"Why can I never say no to you?"

She smiled again and pulled him down to lie with her. Three years of built up need, hurt, anger and passion flowed through them as they took and gave in unison. When all was said and done Alex and Olivia knew this one last time together truly meant something. Their passion was a complete confession of love, and a sincere admittance of differences, somehow holding them together for a lifetime, even if their paths never crossed again.

****

"Get dressed sweetheart, we need to be out of here within the hour so we can make it to John's to get the plane and head to Sitka."

Olivia reluctantly let him go and pulled fresh clothes out of her backpack. They dressed in silence and Alex went outside to finish breaking down the campsite.

While he was cleaning up, Olivia gathered and folded the bedding before making sure they had everything packed and ready to go. Just as she was getting the stuff to take outside, Alex came running into the tent.

"Olivia, how much vacation time do you have?"

"Three weeks, but I already used a week of it and I'm taking my last week immediately after this one so I don't lose..." What Alex was thinking hit her hard.

"Come spend the week with me in Ketchikan," he suggested desperately.

She smiled but still seemed hesitant.

Alex couldn't let this opportunity pass him by. A whole week with Olivia at his home, in his town and she would never leave, he could almost guarantee it. "Come on, it'll be fun. You can explore the town or get to know my friends while I'm at work and we'll have the nights to ourselves. We could even go camping again." Alex sure hoped he hadn't cursed himself with that suggestion, but he thought that maybe, she'd had enough fun this time to want to do it again.

There was no option, she had to do this. "I'd love to spend the week with you. I can't wait to get to know your friends, and I think Pearl and I will get along great."

Alex was counting on it. The more involved she got in his world and with his friends and family, the more she would want to stay. He hoped.

In no time at all, they'd taken the tent down and loaded their stuff on the helicopter. They were leaving their own little paradise and Olivia couldn't help but feel sad as she watched their campground fade into the distance.

The trip from Juneau to Sitka was uneventful and around seven a.m. they landed. Arriving at the docks a short time later, they noticed the ship hadn't arrived yet.

They sat on a bench holding each other and enjoying every minute they had left.

"Alex, come with us today, to the Animal Rehab Center. Please?"

"I'd love to come with you, do you think your parents will mind?"

"Are you kidding? My parents love you, they would probably disown me if I *didn't* invite you."

"Well, we can't have that. Do I need a ticket? I could go buy one right now while we have a bit of time."

"No, my parents are big time donors at this place. This is a complimentary tour so no money is needed."

Alex wrapped his arms tighter around Olivia and looked out at the sea. He couldn't wait to get into his plane again and skim over the water before soaring into the air, he just wished she could be with him this time.

"Hey, look what I see," he said pointing way out into the distance. It was the Sunset Destiny, just coming into view. "They will moor right out there and then use tender boats to bring people ashore. As soon as the first group heads back, you can go back and put your things away and I'll meet you and your family here."

"Okay, be here by ten, the tour starts at eleven or so but dad said to be early."

"I'll be waiting, Doll."

Within the hour, Alex was wandering around Sitka with the rest of the tourists and Olivia was on her way back to the ship. The minute she walked into her cabin, Vanessa pounced. "Come with me Livia, there's a big problem."

"What's wrong?"

"Mari found out about a little piece of Graham's past last night, a little piece from *nine years ago.*"

"What? I thought she already knew about that."

"Well, she didn't. She and Graham have split up now."

"I need to go to her," Olivia sighed, as she threw her backpack on her bed and followed Vanessa down the hall to Jackson's room.

Thank goodness Mari seemed okay, but she was tired of all of the miscommunication between her and Graham so no one knew if their relationship would make it or not.

Olivia and Vanessa comforted their heartbroken sister until it was time to head to the dining room for a family breakfast. Both families ate an awkward meal together, Mari still wasn't talking to Graham and the tension was almost unbearable, before climbing aboard a tender headed for the docks in Sitka.

"Hey mom, I invited Alex to join us. That's okay isn't it?" Olivia asked.

"Of course it is dear, the more the merrier." Her mother's eyes danced in victory but Olivia chose to ignore her, mostly because she was on the verge of being seasick.

At the dock, Olivia felt like it had been way too long since she'd seen Alex even though it had only been an hour and a half. She ran up the ramp and threw herself into his arms, wrapping her legs around him. She was too busy kissing him to notice that her mother high-fived Eleanor and pulled out her cell phone to call her new friend Pearl, in Ketchikan.

They waited an hour for their bus driver to arrive, but it wasn't too bad because she had Alex to talk to and she was able to see some seals frolicking in the water, a first for her. Then a short drive through the rainforest brought them to their destination.

The Center Director, a woman named Jenny, met them and took them on a tour of the facilities. The work they did to rehab animals was so heartwarming and even heartbreaking at times. The group not only saw the public areas, but they were allowed exclusive access to the private areas and were allowed supervised interactions with some of the animals. Olivia's favorite was the injured owl that would soon be transitioned from inside care, to outdoor rehabilitation. Those big owl eyes somehow spoke to her.

"Would you like to name her?" Jenny asked when she saw how attached Olivia had become in such a short time.

"Can I?" she asked excitedly.

"Absolutely!" Jenny answered. "Do you have any ideas?"

Olivia thought for a moment, then whispered something to Alex. When he nodded in the affirmative, she turned to the director. "How about Lily?"

"Perfect!" she enthused before turning away to answer questions from Graham's daughter, Sarah.

Alex hugged Olivia. "That was nice of you to name her after my Grandmother, Doll."

"They're both wise and pulled me into their hearts with their lovely eyes. How could I not?"

Alex kissed her, then told her how much it meant to him. This was the Olivia he'd fallen in love with, not the bitter, scared woman she'd become. She was finally back, one-hundred percent. He just wondered how long it would be before *she* realized it.

"Okay folks, that's it for my part of the tour." Jenny informed them. "I'm going to turn you over to one of our animal experts and he'll take you outside to visit some of our permanent residents."

A man of about thirty walked up to them and smiled. "Hi everybody, I'm Jesse and the first thing I would like to do is to take you out to see our bald eagle Spartan. He is our oldest resident and because of his injuries, he will never be able to leave here." They all gathered together and headed outside to meet the famous Bald Eagle.

Jesse gave them a lesson on eagles and when he said four little words, Olivia's world tilted on its axis. *They mate for life. They mate for life. They mate for life.* The words echoed in her head and she remembered something Alex had said on Mt. Roberts. *"You'll know exactly what makes you happy, what makes you complete. It might be a career, or a hobby, or just a place you like to be. It could be more than one thing. You will feel it deep down in your soul and there will be no mistaking it."*

It was an instantaneous realization, there was no denying it now. She had to be with Alex. He was her eagle and she was his. They were destined to be together forever. Her world was only complete if joined with his.

The thought of giving up her life as a future restaurant owner with a custom home overlooking the lake didn't seem scary anymore, it seemed like the only option. It just felt right. She couldn't wait to tell Alex. But it had to be perfect. She didn't want anyone interrupting them so she would wait until they were alone, and luckily she wouldn't have to wait long.

When the tour ended, the bus took them back to the docks and everyone went their separate ways. Olivia and Alex still had to decide what they wanted to do next. They contemplated walking the trails of Sitka National Historic Park and seeing totem poles carved right there in the forest, and walking through town to explore Sitka's Russian history. Olivia suggested the historic park because she figured they had a better chance of catching some alone time there, they were bound to find a deserted trail somewhere.

About a half hour after returning to the dock, they boarded a shuttle for the State Park. Olivia sat by the window and spent most of the trip looking out at the passing scene, but when they were close to their destination, she decided it was time to start talking with Alex. "I have something I want to tell you when we're alone."

"Okay," he agreed. "No hints?" This would probably be the *'I've had a great time Alex, but I just can't give up my boring, horrible life so I won't be spending the next week in Ketchikan with you'* talk. He'd been dreading it all day even though he'd thought for sure she was finally coming around. He didn't want to say goodbye yet, he never wanted to say goodbye to her again.

"No hints, but you can stop looking like someone punched you in the crotch," she laughed. "It isn't bad." Her eyes danced as she contemplated telling him what she'd decided.

He relaxed and even had a smile on his face when they left the shuttle bus, hand in hand, walking down some of the wood lined pathways, and taking in the intricately carved totem poles. Olivia had never seen such amazing craftsmanship and she couldn't stop raving about them. Alex offered to take her to Totem Bight State Park just outside of Ketchikan while she was visiting. She couldn't wait to see it... and Alex's life.

"Are we alone enough to talk now?" Alex asked, stopping her along the path. There was only one other couple around and they were quite a ways ahead of them.

"Yeah, let's get off the path here. We can sit down on that big rock over there," she said, excited.

Olivia couldn't wait to tell Alex what she wanted to do. Hell, after she told him, she would have a hard time not shouting it from the rooftops.

"So, what did you want to tell me?" he hedged.

She smiled at him. "I don't want to go home. At all. I want to be with you."

Alex sat in silence, stunned. He just stared at her, blinked a few times and then smiled. "You don't know how happy I am to hear that, Doll." But then his voice turned serious. "Are you absolutely sure? Did this just come out of the blue?"

"It really didn't," she assured. "It started at my townhouse the day we left for this trip. My friend Jeff called me a bitch and two minutes later so did Jackson." She chuckled. "It kind of hit home that I really was being horrible to everyone, the question was, why I was like that." She grabbed Alex's left hand. "I pushed the thoughts aside, telling myself that I was successful and happy so nothing else mattered. Then later that night when we were on the ship and I was looking out at the scenery, for the first time ever, I really paid attention and appreciated what I saw." She squeezed his hand and looked him in the eyes. "That's when I realized these little bits of doubt had started to creep into my mind over the last few months. I actually started to wonder if I was truly happy. Of course, I didn't spend too much time thinking about it because I was afraid of the truth. Why ruin a good thing, you know?" She took a deep breath as he brought her hands to his lips and kissed them.

"Oh Alex, you wouldn't believe everything it finally took to make me realize how unhappy I really was."

"Tell, me." he encouraged.

"It took pep talks from Jackson and Vanessa, being here in Alaska and realizing that I never want to leave this paradise, and most of all it took *you*. Admitting that I'm not happy in my current life was the hardest thing I've ever done. But it was the best thing too. I realized on the tour that if we have a life together, I would finally feel complete. It was just like you said, when it happened, I knew it immediately, beyond a shadow of a doubt."

Alex kissed her and didn't let her say anything else until they came up for air.

"So will you have me if I just pack up and move to Ketchikan to be with you?" she questioned.

"Of course I'll have you, I want nothing more." His look suddenly turned serious though. "I want you to go back onto the ship and make double, triple sure that this is what you want. I want this move to be permanent. I don't want you getting to Ketchikan and getting homesick, and leaving me again. I couldn't take it, Livia. We have to know for sure that this will be forever."

"I think I can handle that." She smiled. "Hell, if I tell my family what I'm planning, by the time I get back to Nevada to pack up my stuff and sell my house, they'll have it all done for me." Olivia imagined Charlotte standing there in her townhouse with a clipboard in one hand and a bull whip in the other, shouting orders to the whole family.

Alex gathered her in his arms and held her. He dreamed about the amazing possibilities of their life together. They soon decided to head back into Sitka on the next shuttle so they would have time to explore the town too. Alex was interested in Russian history and wanted to see some of the old buildings and artifacts.

Their self-guided tour and lunch didn't take long, so they decided to just sit at the dock and enjoy each other's company, but before they knew it, it was time to say goodbye.

"I don't want to leave you, Alex. Can't we just fly back to Ketchikan together *now*? My mom can send me my luggage."

"Oh no, don't you tempt me, Living Doll. Please. You really do need to go be by yourself and think over what we talked about earlier. I want this to be perfect."

"I know, I know, it doesn't make saying goodbye any easier though."

He kissed her, lingering a moment before pulling away. "I'll pick you up in Seward at the docks and then we'll fly *home* together."

"Okay," she whispered.

"Hey, don't even think about crying, Love. It's only one and a half days. Besides, I might start if you start."

Olivia smiled then kissed him as if she might not see him ever again. Alex reluctantly broke the kiss. "Just call me if you need anything. Even if you just want to talk," he whispered.

"Okay, Alex," she said quietly. "Goodbye." She reluctantly pulled away from him. The only thing that still touched were their hands and she started to turn away but he pulled her back for one last kiss. "See you soon, Living Doll." And then the attendant helped her onto the tender and she was gone.

****

Alex saw Olivia's brother in-law Graham on the dock so he figured he would say a quick hello to him before calling Pearl to let her know their plans. It turned out that Graham needed a lift to Seward and Alex was more than happy to have the company.

While Graham was getting his stuff off the ship, Alex found a quiet spot and hit speed dial for the office.

"Thank you for calling Paige Air tours, how can I direct your call?"

"Pearl it's me."

"Well, well, how did the camping trip go?"

"Great. Better than I expected," he answered.

"What's the plan now?" Pearl wanted to know.

"Well, she's going to be on the ship until Friday and then we will both be flying home," he told her. "I'm finally bringing her home, Pearl."

"Both of you, together, for good?" Pearl double checked. She had so much hope in her voice.

"Yes, Pearl. She says it's what she wants, but I told her to take the time on the ship without me to talk to her family and make sure this is absolutely, positively what she wants." Alex sounded just as hopeful as his aunt did. "I'm pretty confident in the outcome though, she really has changed."

"That was a very smart thing to do, Alex. I don't want to see either of you with a broken heart again."

"Thanks auntie! Could you let Alice into the house to give it a good cleaning? I want everything to be perfect when we get there."

"Of course I can dear, and don't call me auntie again brat," she joked. "I have one more question before we end this call though."

Should he be nervous? "What question?" he asked reluctantly.

"Have you told her that you aren't just a pilot, that you own this whole place and that you single handedly doubled the profits in less than two years?" she asked calmly.

"No, I wanted to wait until our trip home. That way I would know for sure that she wanted me for me, and not because she thinks I suddenly have a future."

"Okay, I think that'll work. I just hope she doesn't get angry at you for keeping it from her. I'll see you in a few days, Alex."

"Bye Pearl."

A half an hour later, Graham arrived on the docks and they were off to Seward. The flight turned out to be a very interesting one. According to Graham, Olivia's mother Charlotte was responsible for him meeting up with her again. In fact, Charlotte Mannon was responsible for setting up all of her daughters on the cruise. Alex wasn't too sure how he felt about that at first, but then he realized that without Charlotte, he wouldn't have Olivia back. He guessed he could forgive and forget her meddling just this once. And Graham found out that Alex had been on the Animal Rehab Center tour with them. He'd been so involved with trying to reconcile with Mari that he hadn't even noticed.

Alex was happy, with any luck he'd not only found Olivia again, but he'd found a way to reconnect with his old friends.

Once he was safely in his hotel room, what Pearl had said earlier still ran through his mind. Would Olivia really be angry that he didn't mention his ownership of Paige Air Tours? He sure hoped not. She really wouldn't have anything to be angry at. He finally decided that most likely she would be thrilled and then he put the thought out of his mind for good.

Chapter 10

Olivia's original plan had been to talk to her family at dinner that night, but not everyone was present. Mari showed up, then pulled a disappearing act when she found out Graham wasn't on the ship anymore. And Ethan was getting fed up with Charlotte's matchmaking so he left to eat alone in the Café Wave. Now, she would have to talk to everyone individually, unless she wanted to wait until dinner the following night, which she didn't.

The worst thing about talking to everyone individually, was that she didn't want to be alone with her mother when she told her that the matchmaking plan from hell had worked, at least for one of the couples. She couldn't bear to see her mother gloat. Maybe if she started with Jackson, she could convince him to go with her when she told Charlotte. It sure couldn't hurt to ask.

Olivia quietly prayed that her twin would answer her knock, and when he did, she sent a quick thank you upward. "I need to talk to you," she said, pushing past him and seating herself on the loveseat.

"Okay, so talk," he said, sitting next to her.

She couldn't bring herself to look at him. She suddenly realized that he might gloat too. "Are you ready to say I told you so?"

"I won't say that," he laughed. "What did I tell you so about?"

"I do hate my life Jackson, you were so right. I don't know where in the hell I got this warped sense of what I want from life. But I can't do it anymore when all I really want is Alex. Deep down, I know I've wanted only him from the day I met him."

Jackson smiled, "I think I know where you got that warped sense of what you want from life. Mom and I talked about it last night and I think we came up with something."

"Okay then, tell me." She was confused, there was nothing she could bring to mind that would have made her become so warped.

"Remember when we were twelve?" he asked. "And you thought your friend Henry was taking up too much of your time. You said he was getting too needy, that he wouldn't do anything without you?" Jackson stopped there and let Olivia's mind fill in the rest.

Getting tired of Henry always wanting to have her be there for him, she had refused to go to the lake with him and his family. Later that day, while his parents were arguing on the gravel beach, Henry had gone swimming alone and drowned.

"Oh God Jackson," she mumbled.

"You changed after that Liv. That day you said that if you had gone with him he could have relied on you to keep him safe, and by the next morning, you acted like you never wanted to rely on anyone ever again." Jackson put a comforting hand on his twin's arm. "And any kind of weakness in that area made you absolutely furious. A person could only rely on themselves, and no one else."

"How could I have been so blind, Jack? In my mind, anyone who wasn't self-sufficient or who had no plans to make sure that they were self-sufficient was someone I didn't want to be around." She dropped her head into her hands. "And then I met Alex and fell in love with him anyway, but I just couldn't keep it going, this craziness was more important than my love for him. How in the hell did I get so messed up?"

"It turned into a fear Livia, and that's why you couldn't let it go, even for the man you love. Fear is overwhelmingly powerful."

"I know. I never thought of myself as weak, but I was, and my main weakness was the most powerful one – fear. And I realized that it wasn't that Alex didn't have ambition, it's just that he hadn't found what made him complete yet." She'd been '*success above all else*' and Alex had been '*happiness above all else.*'

"You shouldn't be afraid sis, if you love someone, you make it work *together*. Just because you rely on Alex to help you pay the mortgage, doesn't mean you couldn't do it alone if you had to, as long as you're happy," Jackson stressed. "And just because Henry usually relied on you doesn't mean that he died because you weren't there for him that *one* time. It wasn't your fault Liv, do you see what I mean?"

Olivia smiled at her twin. "Oh yeah, I see that now. I guess maybe that's why I didn't want you to pay rent to me. I wanted to prove that I could make the mortgage payment without a roommate's help." She sighed in relief. "So much of what I've done in the past twelve years is clearer now." She leaned over and hugged her brother. "Thank you so much Jackson."

He hugged her back. “So, when do you move?”

“I’m not sure yet. Alex thought it was best that I come back here to think things over, to make sure this is really what I want. If by the time we get to Seward, I feel the way I do now, then I’ll go to Ketchikan for a week and then fly home to sell the townhouse and get my stuff.” A wave of excitement washed over her. “Wow, just saying that gives me goose bumps.” She knew she wouldn’t need to do much thinking about things though. Now that she knew why she was the way she was, it all seemed so silly and she had no doubts whatsoever about staying in Alaska with Alex.

“Well, I know a great realtor when you’re ready to sell. And if you want to, you could give someone in the family power of attorney and you wouldn’t have to hang around too long. You could be living in bliss with Alex all the sooner.”

“Great idea! You’re the best twin a girl could have.” She exclaimed. “Now, I have one more favor to ask you.”

“Okay, ask away.”

“Can you come with me to tell mom and dad? I don’t feel like facing her gloating alone.” Jackson just laughed and pulled her off the loveseat and out the door.

Charlotte and Ethan were just arriving at their suite when Olivia and Jackson saw them.

"Hey, I have something I need to tell you. Can we come in?" Olivia inquired.

"Of course my dear," Ethan said as he unlocked the door for them. "Come in."

Olivia seated herself on the suite's couch and Jackson sat next to her.

"I've got some news," she told them, looking away to avoid Charlotte's piercing gaze. "You win mother, Alex and I are staying together and I'll be moving to Ketchikan." Olivia quickly closed her eyes to protect herself from her mother's glib expression. Later, Jackson would tell her that the only way to describe it was *triumphant*.

"Oh dear, I'm so happy for you!" Charlotte enthused. "You two were meant to be and I'm so glad you found each other again."

"Yes dear, I'm happy for you too," Ethan agreed. "I hope you both will be happy."

Olivia smiled because despite her mom's gloating expression, she knew her parents were truly happy for her. If anyone taught her mother a lesson about her matchmaking, it would have to be someone else because she was just way too happy.

“We’ll go over details later,” Olivia informed them. “As soon as I have more information.”

“Sounds wonderful dear. Just let me know if you need any help and we’ll be glad to pitch in.”

“Thank you mama,” she smiled, and then she and Jackson beat a hasty retreat.

****

Olivia decided to spend some time making plans for her big move so she grabbed a notebook and pen and headed for the ship’s library where she knew it would be quiet. Steven, her shipboard date, was leaving the room just as she was arriving. “Hello, Olivia.”

“Oh, hi Steven!”

“You look happy, did you figure out what you needed to figure out?”

“Yeah I did,” she replied. “I’m back with my ex and I’m going to be moving to Ketchikan soon.” Somehow, she felt like she owed him an explanation.

“Sometimes they aren’t meant to be exes are they,” he said sounding sympathetic. Thank goodness he didn’t sound mad or bitter. “So, moving to Ketchikan huh?” he said nodding his head. “You seemed like a city girl through and through, but you seem different now. I’m happy for you.”

"Thank you, and you're right, that's who I used to be," she lamented. "But not anymore." She walked into the library, waving goodbye to him.

****

In the morning, Olivia woke feeling downright giddy. She had about twenty four hours until she would see Alex again and could give him her decision. She almost couldn't stand the thought of waiting that long to speak to him. She was excited to finally be so absolutely sure about what she really wanted. And to top things off, she'd had the dreams again, both on the same night, but this time it was very different. For the first time, she actually remembered the first dream.

Instead of blowing Henry off when he asked her to go to the lake with his family, she said yes. They swam, had lunch and were building rock castles on the beach when his parents started to argue. Henry didn't want to hear it so he begged Olivia to go swimming with him again. She reluctantly agreed and then all of a sudden they were at a funeral. Olivia was wandering around the cemetery at her current age. Her parents were there, her siblings were there, and her grandparents, aunts and uncles were there. They were all crying. It hadn't made any sense at first. Why was her whole family at Henry's funeral? And then she realized...it wasn't just Henry that was being mourned. Her family was mourning her death too. And then Henry walked up beside her, overlooking the two empty, but soon to be full, graves. "It's okay Olivia, be glad you weren't with me, you would have died too." He turned to her for a hug. "Always remember, it was by no means your fault that I died. Go on and live your life. Love, live, be passionate about everything. Have a good life my friend." And then he disappeared. Olivia woke from that dream feeling refreshed and knowing that her life was finally on the right track after twelve long years. For the first time, the dream hadn't scared her.

When she fell back to sleep, the second dream followed, only this time Alex didn't disappear. She found him, they kissed and he stayed with her.

After a refreshing shower, Olivia figured it was finally time to tell her siblings, they would be heading back to Nevada the next day and she wouldn't. She wanted to start with Abigail. Her sister had finally started to relax a bit and have some fun and Olivia wanted to get to know her again. She knocked on Abby's door hoping she wouldn't be interrupting a love session between her sister and Sam. Charlotte's plan seemed to be well on its way to working for the pair too. But when her sister opened the door to let her in, Olivia's heart fell. Abby had her hair back in the tight bun she always used to wear, and her face was blotchy and red. She'd been crying.

"Oh sweetie," Olivia cried out. "What's wrong? Trouble with Sam?"

Abigail nodded and ushered Olivia inside. "I broke it off with him."

"Oh Abby. Why?" Olivia asked. "You guys seemed so good together."

"We are, or were, but I'm just too messed up inside to make him happy. So I set him free."

Olivia grabbed Abigail's arms and forced her to look at her. "Shouldn't he be the one to decide if you are too messed up for him?"

"I'm just saving him time and trouble, Livia," she cried.

"Again Abby, that should be Sam's choice." Olivia took her sister's hand and led her to the loveseat. "I guess I'm just seeing things differently these days. Alex and I are back together and I'm moving to Ketchikan. We are *proof* that love is powerful and can overcome so much. Please give it a chance."

Abigail looked thoughtfully at her little sister. "I've had feelings for him pretty much since we started working together and it was the same for him. But there is so much in my past that makes this so hard, so much that no one but Sam knows about."

Olivia couldn't imagine what her sister was talking about. She couldn't remember anything bad ever happening to Abigail. Although her personality did change drastically a few years back.

"Fight hard sis, fight hard through the bad together and only good will come from it."

"I've been fighting for years Livia, and I'm tired," Abigail whispered. "I don't know how much more I can take."

"My God, Abby, what happened to you?" Olivia wondered.

"I still can't talk about it, Liv. Someday I will, but I'm not ready yet. Please don't push it."

"Of course I won't. But please let Sam help you fight whatever battle you are dealing with. Two are so much stronger than one."

"Maybe," Abigail mouthed in response.

"Come on, wash your face and come to breakfast with me. I'm starving and you need to eat."

Abigail agreed and within ten minutes they were sitting in the Café Wave with plates piled high, enjoying lighter conversation.

"So you think you'll ever come visit me in Ketchikan?" Olivia asked hopefully.

"Absolutely!" Abigail enthused. "I need to make more time for my family. I'm tired of hurting the ones I love."

"Then talk with me Abby," Sam said quietly, settling down next to her. "Can we please talk about this?"

"You two talk and I'm going to go finish my breakfast with brother dear, he just came in." Olivia announced as she grabbed her plate and drink. She walked over to Jackson, steering him to an empty table.

"Sam and Abby need time alone. Hope you don't mind if I join you for breakfast."

"You're my favorite breakfast companion," he smiled. "Besides, I need some advice."

"About what?" Olivia asked.

"I have to tell everyone about Michael today. They leave Alaska tomorrow and I start the hunt for Deborah. Should I go to everyone individually or do it at dinner tonight?"

Olivia chuckled. "I'm sharing my news individually, but I think your news should be given at dinner. I can't wait until everyone finds out about your son. They're gonna love him!"

"Okay, I guess dinner it is then." Jackson smiled at his twin. "Just remember, act surprised."

"I will." Olivia promised. "I'll even ask you questions about what's going on so no one gets suspicious."

"Perfect sis!"

Olivia and Jackson finished their meal in relative silence and went their separate ways. There was still over an hour until they started cruising past the glaciers. And there was a phone call Olivia wanted to make. She dug through her bag and found her phone. She was getting anxious as the ring count approached twenty. She was about to hang up when she heard a click. "Hello Doll."

"Alex." she choked out and she felt a tear drop onto her hand.

"Living Doll, what's wrong?"

The tears were coming faster now and she whispered. "I don't know. I was fine just a minute ago. Maybe I just miss you."

"I miss you too, Livia," he sighed, "so much.

"I just had to hear your voice," she told him, slowly gaining control.

"I was afraid you'd changed your mind," he nearly whispered.

"Never, Alex!" she cried out. "I don't need any more time, I've made my decision, I've talked to most of my family and I'm choosing you. Forever."

"I was hoping you'd say that," Alex exclaimed. "I was having a hard time waiting until tomorrow to hear your decision."

Olivia chuckled. "Well see, you don't have to wait. I love you, Alex. I always have."

"I love you too. I'll see you tomorrow, Livia."

"Bye Alex."

"Olivia, wait!"

"What?"

"Graham is planning something big for Mari in Seward, so I'll have to pick you up after that. Call my cell when you're ready."

"What kind of surprise?" Olivia asked curiously.

"Can't tell you that, Love. Just don't say anything to Mari, okay?"

Olivia sighed. "Okay Alex, I'll see you when I see you."

"Bye my love."

Olivia smiled as she hung up the phone. Now she had two things to be excited about the following day. Her sister was getting a big surprise from her husband, which meant that they would most likely stay together after their little break up. And of course she would get to be with Alex again. Her phone buzzed and she opened the text. *I still love you...forever.* Olivia hit reply, typed the same words back to him and hit send.

****

Olivia was actually excited about dinner. She couldn't wait until Jackson told everyone about Michael. As she dressed, she tried to imagine what everyone would think of the big news. They would rightly be shocked, but most likely supportive too. And Charlotte would be thrilled to have a grandchild. Hell, she'd probably start the hunt for a wife for him right after dinner.

Olivia was the first to arrive at the dining room and Vanessa was second.

"Just the person I wanted to see!" Olivia exclaimed and pulled her sister down next to her. "I've got news," she sang out.

Vanessa laughed. "Let me guess, you and Alex are back together forever and you're leaving the excitement of the Vegas area for the quint charm of Ketchikan, Alaska?"

"Wow, you're good," Olivia exclaimed.

"It's written all over your face, Livia." Vanessa stated. "And I am so unbelievably happy for you!" She pulled her sister into a big hug.

"I'm going to miss you Nessa, but this is definitely the right thing to do." Olivia reassured.

"I'm going to miss you too, but I agree, this is definitely the right thing for you and Alex. You two belong together."

Olivia smiled at her sister but then got serious. "Where's Thomas? You two aren't still fighting are you?"

Vanessa sighed. "Kind of, he's going to give me an answer about the state of our relationship before we leave the ship tomorrow."

"He'll make the right decision sis." Olivia assured.

Vanessa smiled and hugged her sister again. "I hope so, I love him."

One by one everyone else showed up and dinner was ordered. Conversation went on as usual until halfway through the meal, when Jackson stood and asked for everyone's attention. Now they all would know what had been bothering him for the last week. "I have something to tell all of you. It's probably going to be a shock. I've been putting it off this whole trip, but tonight is the last chance, so here goes." He took a deep breath and Olivia saw that he was shaking. "I don't have a lot of details yet, but they think Deborah is in Anchorage or Denali." Everyone gasped so he paused. "She fled there when she left Nevada, to live with her uncle. When he passed away, she disappeared again. Her mom had been searching for her but is now dying of cancer. She has asked me to come find Debra so she can see her one last time before she dies." He paused and looked around the table, trying to judge what everyone was thinking, then he continued. "And it seems there is a little seven year old surprise. His name is Michael Steven Mannon. He's my son."

"So is that why she left?" Olivia asked, acting confused.

"No, from what I understand, she left because she was in danger of some sort. I'm not sure what it was all about, but I *will* find out," he said with determination. "I won't be coming home with all of you, I have to stay on in Anchorage and look for Debra. If I can't find her, I'll bring my son home in time to start school in the fall."

The family was stunned but soon loosened up and were talking about the new family member that they couldn't wait to meet. There would be a celebration! Charlotte even had tears in her eyes at the thought of a grandchild.

Another round of cake and champagne was in order, courtesy of the head waiter of course. It seemed that the further they got into the vacation the more there was to celebrate. But as always, family time had to end and the group was shooed out of the dining room so they could set up for late dining. Everyone went their separate ways, each choosing to spend their last night on the cruise in a special way.

As they left the dining room, Jackson congratulated Olivia on her performance and she hugged her twin. “You’re welcome.”

“I sure am going to miss you. It’ll take some getting used to, not having my twin close by.”

Olivia smacked his chest. “That just means you have to come visit me. A lot!” Olivia enthused. “You could even move there, I’m sure they need Park Rangers in Ketchikan don’t they?”

Jackson chuckled. “I think I’ll stay in Nevada. For now. I’ll come visit you a lot though.”

“Sounds perfect.”

“So what do you have planned for your last night on the cruise?” Jackson asked. “I’m going to try to talk some sense into Thomas over drinks then I’m going to pack. Nothing exciting here.”

Olivia nodded. “I’ll be packing and planning for the move. We are such fun people these days.”

Jackson laughed, “I’ll see you at departure tomorrow. Love ya Sis.”

“I love you too dork!” she called, walking to the elevator.

In the peace of her room she quickly packed her stuff, then sat on her bed and started making list after list of things she needed to do to move to Ketchikan. She fell asleep working on page three and stayed asleep even when Vanessa came in.

A knock at the door at about one a.m., woke both Olivia and Vanessa. And since Vanessa was on the bottom bunk she struggled out of bed and opened the door to Thomas.

When Olivia heard what he had to say, she knew she needed to evacuate the premises. She grabbed a change of clothes and her carry-on bags, traded keys with Thomas and headed to Jacksons cabin. She slept better than she had in years.

Chapter 11

Unlike the others on the cruise with her, Olivia couldn't wait to get off the ship. Not that she hadn't had a great time, because she had, but the best part of her vacation had taken place on land.

The sun was shining bright when she walked across the gangplank. It was a beautiful day in Seward, but it wasn't hot like home would have been. Her old home that is, her new one was probably rainy and cool and she couldn't wait to fly there that afternoon.

Daydreams of the future found her following her family blindly off the ship and she bumped into Jackson when he stopped abruptly in front of her. Peeking around him, she noticed there were two limousines waiting for the Mannon and Blake parties. Whatever her brother-in-law had planned better be damn good because it was postponing her seeing Alex again. The luxury transportation was a good start though, and in the end Olivia wasn't disappointed.

The surprise Graham had for Mari was well worth waiting an extra few hours to see Alex for. Her brother-in-law surprised his wife with a real wedding and reception, with everything including dresses and flowers. Mari finally had her dream wedding and a fun family celebration too. When the happy couple left for their honeymoon, Olivia pulled her cellphone out to call Alex.

"Hello Doll."

"Hi Alex, when do I get to see you?" She asked anxiously.

"I'll be there in fifteen minutes, if you're ready to leave."

"I am. You should have come to the wedding, everyone asked about you."

"I had some business to take care of," he told her. "I wish I could have been there with you though."

"Me too, now just come and get me damn it. I miss you!"

"On my way!"

As the Mannon and Blake families, minus Mari and Graham, walked out of the church, Alex was standing across the street leaning against his rental car. Olivia waved and turned to her family for a round of goodbye hugs before she went to Ketchikan and they headed to the airport in Anchorage. "Thank you mama," she whispered into Charlotte's ear as she hugged her mother tight.

"I'm just glad you're finally happy," Charlotte whispered back.

Olivia pulled away with a smile and ran across the street and into Alex's waiting arms. The cheers and calls from her family made her blush, but she didn't care. When Alex's lips met hers, everything melted away because she was finally *exactly* where she wanted to be.

"Are you ready to start a new life?" Alex asked as he held her.

"I am! Can we go now?" she enthused.

Alex laughed and pulled away from her. "Only if we get into the car."

She swatted at him and ran around to her side, waving one last time across the street to her family. Alex helped Jackson load the luggage into the trunk then slid behind the wheel. They pulled away from the curb and headed out of town, her twin waving until they were out of sight. "So where's your plane?" Olivia asked as she took in the sight of him.

"The seaplane base in Moose Pass. About thirty miles from here."

"Okay, I'm just so anxious to get home, I mean... Yeah, home. Right?"

"Absolutely Doll, *our* home." He smiled at her.

They drove through some beautiful country, and Olivia made commentary on every little thing she saw. "Oh Alex, it's so gorgeous here. Can we come back and visit some time?"

Alex smiled at her again. "Anytime you want, Livia. Just say the word."

She was somewhat sad when the drive to Moose Pass ended, but she also felt like an excited child. There was so much of her new world she couldn't wait to explore, and she was going to enjoy every minute while she still could. Unfortunately soon, they would have to come back down to earth and she would have to find a job.

****

Alex finished loading the plane and Olivia climbed aboard.

"You ready to head home, Doll?'

"Of course I am!" She answered, her voice shaking with excitement. Five minutes later, they were on their way.

The first hour of the flight went quickly as they talked about their future and the plans they had for Olivia to sell her townhome.

"What do you want to do for work, Love?" Alex asked.

"I'm not sure. I'll have to see what's available..." And then something hit her, in the side pocket of her bag was a small blue sales brochure from the diner in Ketchikan. She didn't remember ever picking it up, but when she packed her bag it was there.

"Hey Alex, what do you know about The Dock Stop Diner?"

"I know it has great food, and I know Pearl's best friend Millie owns it," he stated. "Why?"

"Somehow a sales brochure ended up in my bag, and I'm thinking I could use my inheritance to buy it." Excitement shone in her eyes. "I could live my dream of owning my own restaurant!"

Alex looked seriously at Olivia. "It's far from a five star establishment Doll, but if you can live with that, I think it's a great idea."

Olivia smiled at him. "Five star was so last week, Alex. I'm more into Alaskan tourist trap now," she joked.

He smiled back at her. "I think you would love owning that place; great customer base-local and tourist, great people working for you, and I think her price is right on. A shop down the street just sold for double that."

Olivia just nodded and re-read the brochure, excitement building more with every word. Now all she had to do was convince her mother to let her have access to her inheritance a few months early. Officially she wasn't supposed to touch it until her twenty-fifth birthday in November, but Charlotte could give her special permission to use it if needed.

"So who passed away and left you an inheritance?" Alex questioned.

"Oh, I guess I forgot to tell you," she whispered. "My nana Violet died two years ago and left all of us kids some money. Abby has hers, Mari re-invested hers for another two years, Jackson and I get ours in November and Vanessa gets hers in three years when she turns twenty-five."

"You always talked so lovingly of Nana Violet. I wish I'd been able to meet her."

"She would have loved you, Alex." Olivia laughed "I told her all about us, and she called me a ninny for letting you go, I think she knew what she was talking about."

Alex smiled and grabbed her hand to give it a squeeze.

Olivia started to dream about what life would be like for her. They would work as pilot and restaurant owner, they would get married and maybe they would have a couple of kids down the road. The decision was made, her kids would not grow up pampered, they would be out hiking before they could walk. She saw herself carrying them through the forest in one of those baby carriers.

"Why are we getting ready to land, Alex?" Olivia asked when she realized what he was doing.

"Going to add fuel and maybe have dinner with John and Sue, if you're up to it."

"Oh, I'd love to get to know them better!" She exclaimed.

"It's settled then," Alex said excitedly as the plane came to a stop and they stepped out into the cool evening air. "You go buy them a bottle of wine to have with dinner and I'll take care of The *Living Doll* and call John. We'll meet back at the plane in forty minutes. He'll pick us up then."

"How about I take care of The *Doll* for you and you go into town with the lady."

Alex turned and saw John walking towards them. "You don't mind?" Alex asked his friend as they shook hands.

"Not at all. I miss working with the floatplanes," John assured.

"Well okay then, we'll be back in a bit." He grabbed Olivia's hand and they walked toward town.

"Alex, back there, why did you call the plane The *Living Doll*? I thought you were talking about refueling me there for a minute," she joked.

Alex laughed. "I'll refuel you later," he whispered.

Olivia trembled and squeezed his hand. Each moment until they arrived home would be agonizing now.

"When I bought her, I thought she needed a name. She was so temperamental, just like you, so I decided on The *Living Doll*."

"So you named a temperamental airplane after me?" she asked, raising an eyebrow.

"Yeah, are you mad?" He asked.

"No! Actually, I think it is kind of sweet that you loved me enough to do that."

Alex smiled at her. "It's gonna get complicated now. Both of the special ladies in my life have the same name. Are you going to get jealous?"

Olivia played along. "No, there's a lot that I can give you that she can't."

"So true! She's not a very good kisser." Alex joked. "Figuratively you put my head in the clouds and literally she takes me there."

They were both laughing as they stepped into the liquor store.

Helping people pick out wine had been pretty much a daily activity at her job so it didn't take long to pick the perfect one. When she insisted on paying, it reminded Alex that he still hadn't told her how much of a success he actually was. He made a point to tell her as soon as they got home to Ketchikan, and then he would make love to her until neither of them could think straight. They needed to christen his house, now their *home*, in every possible way.

****

Twenty minutes after they made it back to The *Living Doll*, John swung his SUV into his driveway. He was quite the character, who had pretty much been everywhere and done everything. He'd been a friend to Alex's dad and uncle, and was now a father figure and mentor to Alex. Olivia loved him already.

"Welcome, welcome." Sue greeted them at the door. "So glad you guys are here together." She wrapped Olivia in a big warm hug. "Dinner is waiting, follow me."

Olivia presented her host with the bottle of wine and followed her to the dining room. Alex and John weren't far behind.

"Sit down and eat everyone! No formalities at this table, just eat and enjoy."

Olivia took a seat next to Alex and they both filled their plates with a very delicious pasta in white wine sauce and home grown steamed veggies. "This is so good!" Olivia exclaimed. "I swear I've had it before."

"You probably have dear," Sue stated happily. "I got the recipe from Alex."

They ate in silence for a while until the two men began to talk shop. "So, boy, when are you going to scrap those old monster floats you own and get a new fleet?" John asked. "You've done more to advance that business since you've owned it than your uncle did in twenty-five years. Not saying he wasn't a good business man, just that he wasn't much for adding on or making improvements."

The cat was out of the bag. Alex turned slowly to look at Olivia, she'd gone pale and he could see disbelief building in her with every passing second.

"Are you okay, Livia?" Alex asked her, putting a calming hand on her arm.

"You own Paige Air Tours?" she asked quietly.

"Yes," he answered.

"Why didn't you tell me?" She almost looked hurt that he'd kept it from her.

He took her hands in his. "Because I didn't want any of the old crap getting in the way this time. I wanted you to come back to me because you loved me, not because I finally met your expectations."

"I was awful to you, I deserved that," she whispered.

"I just had to protect myself from any possible pain. It nearly killed me, losing you the first time."

"He's right, Olivia. He was a mess for a long time. You should have seen him when we finally got him here after his daddy and uncle died." John just shook his head. "Mess with a capital M he was, and it wasn't all because of the family tragedy."

"I'm so sorry Alex," Olivia cried. "I was so misguided, I..."

"No more apologies, Doll," he said, putting a finger to her lips. "We're finally together and that's all that matters."

"If I were you I'd never speak to me again," she said, wiping the tears from her eyes.

Alex kissed her and pulled her close. When his phone buzzed, they both jumped apart and he pulled it out of his pocket. "Shit! John and Sue, we're going to have to continue this another time. That storm is headed this way quicker than they thought. We need to get going. Now!"

"I'll meet you in the truck," John said.

"We'll come down to visit you sometime this week," Sue informed them as she packaged up some of the dessert they hadn't been able to get to. "And enjoy this when you get home." She pulled first Alex, and then Olivia into a hug and shooed them out the door. Not too much later John dropped them off on the dock and they hurried aboard The Living Doll, headed for home.

****

"That was close!" Alex told Olivia as he handed her a blue rain slicker. "Put this on, and when I get back, hold on to my hand and run like hell for the office. Understand?"

Olivia nodded as she shrugged into the slicker.

"Wait here, I'll be right back. I just have to secure the plane," and he was gone. When he re-appeared, he was soaking wet. "Come on let's go," and he held out his hand to her. She grabbed ahold and stepped out of the plane. The wind and rain hit her hard almost knocking her off her feet. Alex kept her upright as they made a mad dash down the road to the office.

Once safely inside, they noticed Pearl sitting at her desk. "What are you doing here Pearl?" Alex asked, surprised.

"Making sure you two made it okay," she answered. "Welcome home Olivia. I for one am so glad you're here."

"That makes two of us, Pearl," Alex agreed. He excused himself and came back drying his hair with a towel. The two beautiful women in his life had their heads together and were smiling and joking around together. He was warmed by the sight.

Olivia looked up and smiled, the man she loved looked like a drowned rat. "You should have waited to give me the slicker until you secured the plane."

"I would have been soaked when I took it off to give it to you and you would've been soaked when you put it on," he answered. "Didn't want you baptized on your first day here" he joked. "There will be plenty of time for you to get used to the rain."

"The rest of our lives," she said with a smile.

Alex took her into his arms and kissed her. He still had a hard time believing how lucky he was to have found her again.

"Okay, you two, get on home before you embarrass yourselves," Pearl cackled as she waked out the front door.

"She's right. I want to be home when I make crazy hot love to you." Alex lamented. "We'll save the office for another day."

Olivia blushed as she watched Alex walk through the room turning lights off. She couldn't wait to get home now!

A short ride later, they pulled into the driveway of his cozy yellow cottage.

"Welcome home, Living Doll," Alex whispered in her ear right before capturing her mouth in a kiss so hot it instantly steamed up the truck windows. He pulled away breathless. "We should probably get inside before we freeze."

"Yeah," Olivia agreed even though she really just wanted to stay right there and kiss Alex all night long.

"On the count of one...two...three..." They both threw their doors open and ran for the house. Alex unlocked the front door and ushered her inside. "Take the slicker off and make yourself comfortable. I need to get out of these wet clothes and take a hot shower."

Olivia carefully stripped the dripping rain coat off and hung it on the coat rack. Slipping off her wet shoes, she padded over to the couch. Her body sunk into the cushions and she leaned her head back. It was so good to be home. And that was the weird part, she hadn't even seen all of this house yet, but she felt more at home here than she ever had in her own townhouse.

When she finally heard the shower turn on, the thought of being with Alex was too hard to ignore so she decided to join him. She stripped out of her clothes, leaving them on the easy chair in the corner of the bedroom and walked into the master bathroom.

"Alex," she called out.

"Come on in Doll, the water's perfect."

She slid the shower door open and stepped inside. Alex enveloped her with his strong, muscular, oh so naked physique. "Needed to get warm too huh?" he whispered.

"Clean and warm," she replied. "Thought we could conserve water," She reached out to run her fingers lightly over his abdomen. The sight of his body reacting to her touch made her smile and she took ahold of him running her hand up his length.

He let out a low hiss "I thought shower sex wasn't your favorite," he ground out.

"Hmm you're right, it isn't. Maybe we should just wash each other and move this party elsewhere."

"You just like teasing me to the brink of insanity," he said softly, as he rubbed shower gel over her chest and stomach.

"There's that too," she whispered, becoming lost in the sensation of his hands working her body. As he washed her, she washed him and it was hard to tell if the steam in the shower was caused by the hot water or the heated, slick bodies teasing and being teased by water, gel and exploring hands.

Alex gently grabbed Olivia's arms and held them tight. "No more Doll, or we won't make it to the bed."

"We have all night Alex." Olivia reminded him with a sly smile, as she pulled her hands free. "I didn't get to finish what I started the last time I was here. I will this time."

Alex took in a deep breath and relaxed as her hand wrapped around him again. She was going to do what she wanted and he was going to love every minute of it. He leaned back against the shower stall and moaned as her hand started to move. His hips pressed into her and she released him, running her fingers down his thighs. She knelt in front of him, the warm water running down her back as she grasped him again. This time she didn't stroke until she took him into her mouth too. She ran her tongue around the head and moved her hand vigorously at the same time, stopping only occasionally to take him all the way in.

"Jesus Doll, it's been so long..." he groaned.

She had him so close. Increasing her pace, her hand and mouth working together, she gave him what he needed, what he'd wanted for three long years.

"Now Doll," he gasped.

She stopped moving and squeezed bringing him to the end of the ride, accepting all he had to give her.

Pulling away, she sat back, letting the now cool water wash over her and take some of the heat from her body.

With one hand, he pulled Olivia to her feet and with the other, he turned off the water. She followed him out of the shower stall and caught the towel he tossed to her.

She started to dry off and Alex followed suit, his eyes never leaving her. "Do you like watching me?" she asked, softly.

"More than almost anything," he groaned. "Here, let me." He took her towel and gently turned her around to dry her back. "I love your hair like this, it fits you."

"I knew you'd like it, that's why I cut it this way, three days after we broke up," she mumbled, trying to control the fire that burned through her with every touch.

When she felt his lips on her shoulder and he pulled her back against him, she jumped a little. His lips and then his tongue traced a path from her shoulder to her neck and she screeched, then laughed, when Alex scooped her up and carried her to their bed.

He slid down beside her and captured her mouth. His hands caressed her hip while his tongue teased her lips. A moan escaped her, the feeling of familiarity driving her mad.

Her hand branded him from hip to waist and around to his back where her nails dug in when he gently squeezed a nipple between two fingers. She stopped kissing him abruptly and he knew exactly what she wanted. He moved his mouth to her breast and teased her into a sigh, with his tongue making short hot strokes on her nipple and down the side of her breast, just how she liked it.

"You remember," she exclaimed with a shiver. He didn't answer, he just did it again, this time dipping his hand past her abdomen to the folds that welcomed first one and then two fingers inside. He pressed firmly into her, resting the heel of his hand on her most sensitive spot. She arched her back, pulling him deeper and increasing the pleasure. With his hand pressed into her, the feeling was so intense, she had to force herself to relax and pull back.

"Alex, not yet," she cried.

“Now, Olivia,” he said, moving his hand in a circular motion. “If I remember correctly there can be many more where this came from.” Her body shuddered as her muscles clenched around his fingers.

He adjusted himself over her as she pulled him into a kiss. Her hips lifted in invitation and he slid inside, slow and shallow. He pulled back and she whimpered. He pushed in again a bit farther this time, and she sighed. He moved again for only a few fleeting moments then pulled back, hovering over her. “It’s my turn to tease you.”

“Alex, please!”

“No,” and he slid in slow and shallow again until she sighed. He stopped moving, hearing her familiar whimper. The next time he thrust forward, he gave her a glimpse of what she’d asked for and she met him eagerly. “I’m taking it nice and slow tonight Love, so relax and enjoy the ride.”

Olivia looked into his eyes. “Show me what you’ve got,” she whispered through clenched teeth.

Alex moved slow and deep while teasing her breasts with his fingers and her lips with his tongue. Just when he sensed she was about to lose her mind, he stopped, only to start slowly again a moment later. He brought her to the brink, again and again.

"Oh my God Alex, please." She gasped. He increased his pace, moving in as deep as he could go, and her legs wrapped around his waist, moving with him. The more firm his hold on her, the stronger the sensation. Heat built and spread through her body and when the flames of desire consumed all of her, she called out his name. He fell over the edge to the sound of her pleasure filled voice.

"Alex?" Olivia questioned as he lifted himself off of her, pulling her close to his side.

"Yes?"

"You're mean!"

He laughed and Olivia relished every note. She'd missed his laugh so much. After sending him away she would lie in bed on weekend mornings and wait for his laughter to waft in from the kitchen where he would read the comics or joke around with Jackson. When the sound never came, she was always incredibly sad.

"Well, if I'm mean then I assume you didn't enjoy yourself?" he asked absently rubbing the very sensitive spot at the underside of her breast.

"I didn't say that!"

He smiled at her. "So does that mean we can do it again sometime?" he asked hopefully.

"And again, and again, and again," she answered right before he kissed her.

"I love you so much, Olivia."

"I love you too, Alex. Will you ever be able to completely forgive me?" she hedged. She wasn't sure if she wanted to hear the answer but knew she had to.

"I forgave you years ago," he promised. "It's hard to explain, but I finally realized that the Olivia who broke up with me wasn't the real you. Unfortunately, I didn't think the real you could ever exist again. But when I saw you last week, I knew I had to try to bring the woman I fell in love with back to me."

"Thank God it worked!" she exclaimed with a smile. "And I'm so glad that all those years ago you were able to differentiate between the real me and the completely messed up me."

"When I fell in love with you, that first day we met, I think it was too hot outside for you to be anything but the real you." Alex reflected.

Olivia chuckled. "Yeah, you're right when it's that hot you can't put up walls, you just try to survive."

"Exactly," he smiled, caressing her thigh.

"Alex?"

"Yeah?"

"Unless you're ready to go again, I suggest you stop touching me like that."

Alex left his hand right where it was.

Chapter 12

Olivia woke to the sound of laughter, Alex's laughter, and the enticing aroma of bacon and French toast. Her suitcase was by the nightstand when she slid out of bed so she grabbed her robe and slippers out, put them on and hurried into the kitchen.

"Good morning," she called almost shyly as she pushed through the swinging door. "What were you laughing at?"

Alex looked up from the stove and smiled. "Good morning Doll, I was on the phone with Pearl. I hope cinnamon french toast with bacon and eggs is still your favorite breakfast."

"It is!" she smiled. "And I'm starving."

"Go sit down in the dining room. I'll bring it right out."

"Okay," she walked back out to the dining room and took a seat at the small two person table, the door creaked and then thumped behind her.

"I think it's time to bring the full sized dining set in from the garage," he suggested as he dropped a kiss on the top of her head and set her plate in front of her. "Breakfast is served."

"Oh yum. It looks perfect as always," she gushed "I'm not sure how I even ate again after you left."

"You're a flatterer."

"No really Alex, if you ever had to give up flying you could come cook for me at my restaurant," she joked.

"Probably not a good idea sweetheart. I can barely keep my hands off of you. We'd spend more time fooling around in the kitchen than we would working."

"True," she agreed. She knew it wasn't really possible, but it didn't stop her from wanting to make up for every last day they'd been apart. The daydream took over all conversation and they ate in silence for a while. Olivia was the first to break it.

"So what are we doing today?"

"Well, after breakfast I thought you could come with me to the staff meeting at Paige Air Tours, then I could show you around town, find you a vehicle to use, introduce you to Millie and then I have a surprise for you. After all that I thought we could go to dinner and come home to recreate last night." He winked at her, then stood and gathered their dishes. He stopped to kiss her before walking into the kitchen. Then again, maybe they wouldn't make it out the door on time.

****

The first thing Alex did was take Olivia to the office to meet Jason and Mark. The weekly staff meeting had to go on even if the boss was still technically on vacation.

Olivia sat in on the meeting, at first she felt a bit awkward but then she just sat there mesmerized. This was a whole new Alex she was witnessing, he was self-confident in his work ability, he was completely in charge, and best of all he was happy. Talking about logistics and marketing didn't make him miserable in the least. She'd never seen him this content with his job and Mark and Jason seemed to adore him. They respected him greatly, it was the perfect working relationship.

When the meeting finally wound down, formal introductions were made "And guys, I would like you to meet my ex..." He turned to Olivia and pulled her close to his side. "... My *girlfriend* Olivia Mannon. Olivia this is Jason Schreiber and Mark Jenkins, the two best pilots, and friends around."

"So you're the original, Living Doll." Mark enthused, taking her hand. "It's so great to finally meet you, and I must say you are much prettier than that old plane."

Jason pushed Mark out of the way to take his turn greeting his best friend's love. "It's so nice to meet you. We've heard nothing but great things from Alex." He pulled her closer and whispered, "He loves you very much."

Olivia felt herself blush, it really warmed her heart to hear that and it made her know for sure that she'd made the right decision. "It's nice to meet both of you."

"So, how do you like Ketchikan so far?" Mark inquired.

"I love it! At least what I've seen," she answered. "And I'm sure it'll be even better once I've had the chance to explore and meet some people."

"If you want to meet people, just come on over to my house tonight at seven," Jason told her. "Our wives," he said pointing to Mark, "and a bunch of other ladies take over the house to hang out and work on community projects while all of the men escape to the garage."

"And maybe you can convince Mr. Anti-social to come on over again too," Mark interjected.

"Can we, Alex? I want to meet your friends," Olivia asked, getting excited at the prospect.

"Of course," he answered with a smile. "I stopped going when I started working on something big for the business, but that's almost over so I think I can go back now."

Everyone in the room looked at Alex curiously and he felt the weight of the stares. "Don't worry, it's all good and you'll all know about it soon. I just have a few details to work out." Everyone trusted Alex enough to take his words at face value, with no extra discussion or prodding for details. Olivia couldn't help but marvel at how good Alex was with his employees. She always knew he had the makings of a successful boss, it just took the right kind of job. Alex was born to work at something he loved, not at something chosen out of necessity. The guilt for how she'd treated him, for all the times she'd doubted him, felt suffocating all of a sudden. Pearl grabbed her in a hug when the men stepped outside. "It's okay sweetie, it all worked out. No more guilt."

Olivia welcomed Pearl's motherly embrace. "It's hard not to feel guilty. I hurt the man I love and wasted so much precious time."

"You're young, you can make up for that time and just look at Alex," she said, pointing out the windows. "He's far from hurting now."

Olivia studied Alex and realized that Pearl was right, he was truly happy and she'd never seen him like that before.

"I know what's going through your mind kiddo and you need to stop." Pearl warned. "He was happy he finally found a job he loves, but there was always still something missing until you came here."

"I've never seen him like this Pearl."

"I haven't either darlin, I haven't either."

The two women were hugging again when Alex poked his head in the door. "Ready to go, Doll?"

Olivia pulled away from Alex's aunt. "Thanks Pearl."

"Anytime sweetie."

"What was that about?" Alex asked with a smile on his face. It seemed Olivia and Pearl were bonding already and that made him happy. They were the only family he had left. At least he hoped Olivia would officially be family soon.

"I was feeling guilty again and she set me straight."

"Good, nothing to be guilty about, Love." Alex backed her up against the passenger side of his truck and kissed her. His hands made their way up under her hoodie to caress her sides. They didn't even think of stopping what they were doing until they heard the office door slam shut.

"Okay, let's get out of here," Alex suggested. "Before Pearl tells us to get a room and I drag you off to do just that," he sighed. "We have a lot to do today."

"What's next?" Olivia asked as she climbed up into the truck.

Alex ran around to his side and got in. "Next stop, Aunties house," he hollered out his open window.

"I heard that boy!" Pearl hollered back on the way to her car.

Alex laughed and started the truck.

Olivia wondered why they were going to Pearl's house but she didn't ask, she was content to look out the window at her new town. It wouldn't take her long to know her way around. It only took them five minutes to get there and when they rounded the corner, Pearl's house came into view. Olivia couldn't believe her eyes, Alex's aunt had a fabulous house with a killer water view.

"Oh Alex, what a great house!" she exclaimed. "And look at that view!"

"I'm glad you like it. In fact it's very important that you do."

"But why?" Olivia asked, her curiosity getting the better of her.

"You'll see," was all he said.

They pulled into the driveway and Alex opened the garage with a remote from inside his truck. "I don't know what you had planned as far as vehicles go, but if you don't want to ship your car over here, you can have my second car."

The garage opened up to a gun metal gray Jeep, exactly like the one she had at home.

"My uncle had just bought it when he died. I only use it when I have to take clients somewhere, so if you want it, it's yours."

"Oh Alex, it's perfect! Let's go look at it," she exclaimed.

Alex raced her to the car and unlocked it for her. She climbed in and he handed her the key. "Start it up, Doll."

Olivia stared the vehicle and revved the engine. She absolutely loved this kind of car and this one would be perfect. It was the same year as hers, but when she checked the mileage she was flabbergasted. "Alex, this only has 1200 miles on it."

He shrugged, "like I said, it was mainly for taking clients around in. It's just wasting away here, so we might as well get some use out of it."

She turned the engine off and stepped out of the vehicle. "Thank you so much, Alex. That's one big worry, and expense, off of my mind."

"Don't need to thank me," he reminded her. "Let's go see the house." He led her in through the inside garage door.

The house was absolutely grand. It was two stories with a winding staircase with dark wood banisters. The great room was comfortable yet elegant and the kitchen was a chef's dream.

"I bet you love the kitchen, don't you, Alex?"

"You bet, it's my favorite room in the house." He smiled and his eyes twinkled. "I'll show you my favorite outdoor space too. Come on." He led her out to a deck that spanned the width of the house and looked out over the water.

Olivia walked over to the railing and took in the horizon view. "I could stand here all day."

Alex walked up behind her and wrapped his arms tightly around her waist.

"So could I," he whispered in her ear. "But only with you by my side."

Olivia turned in his arms and kissed him. She was in paradise with the man she loved. She was counting her blessings for sure, but she couldn't help but have the fleeting thought that knowing her luck, it would all come crashing down around her. She pushed the negative thoughts away when Alex broke the kiss and led her to a small outdoor table set for two.

"I thought maybe we could eat lunch out here and enjoy the view a bit longer."

"Sounds perfect," she agreed as she sat in the chair Alex held out for her.

"This meal should bring back memories," he told her as Pearl's housekeeper, Alice, set plates in front of them.

"Vegetable omelets and rye toast. You made me this exact meal after we made love all morning and into the afternoon on the day you returned from Seattle. Exactly a week after our first time," Olivia reminisced. Looking up at Alex, she noticed he seemed preoccupied.

"Yeah, I decided to have Alice make you something special because I'm hoping this will be an afternoon to remember, just like that one was."

Olivia studied his face. He looked almost shy, somehow unsure of himself and that wasn't like Alex at all. "What do you mean?" she asked.

"Let me say what I need to say all at once so I don't lose my courage okay?"

"Of course, go ahead, I promise I won't interrupt." She was even more curious now, and even a bit anxious.

"The day we broke up, I had planned to ask you to marry me. I had hoped that somehow, by committing to you, it would make you believe I was capable of making something last." He chuckled bitterly. "But you broke up with me before I could do it."

Olivia could still see the pain shadowed in his eyes. She'd promised him she wouldn't interrupt so she just reached over and squeezed his hand, hoping it was enough.

"I had the ring and everything." He smiled as if remembering something good. "I told Grandma Lily what I wanted to do and she gave me her rings to give to you. By then, she was terminal and knew that she wouldn't need them much longer. She told me she loved you and that we reminded her of herself and Grandpa."

Olivia felt tears spring into her eyes and run down her face. Grandma Lily was a wonderful woman. They'd become close while she and Alex were dating. She'd heard that Lily and her husband, Jefferson, had died within days of each other, her from cancer and he from what everyone said was a broken heart. She still felt guilty for not going to the funerals, but she'd been too afraid of running into Alex. A donation to their favorite charity had to suffice.

Alex reached out and wiped the tears from her cheeks. "When we didn't work out I vowed never to use the rings because in my mind they were yours, and yours only." He stood and held his hand out to her, leading her over to the railing to look out at the water again. Pulling her close, they kissed, almost form instinct, neither one giving thought or planning to it, then he held her tight for just a moment.

"Olivia, I love you so much, I always have," he said reaching into his pocket and stepping back. "Will you accept my grandmother's rings? One today to mark our engagement and one on the day of our wedding? I want to spend the rest of my life with you, please marry me?"

The tears were back, this time however, they were tears of joy. "Yes Alex, I'll marry you." She wrapped her arms tightly around him. "I'm so honored that your Grandmother wanted me to have her rings. I think she knew we were supposed to be together."

"I think so too," he agreed, taking the engagement ring out of the box and slipping it on her finger. "I had it sized three years ago, I'm just glad it still fits because I want you to wear it starting right this minute, through forever."

They were kissing again when Pearl walked out onto the deck. "I take it she said yes?" Pearl hedged, hoping that Alex had actually proposed already and she wasn't spoiling anything.

Alex raised his arm above his head and gave Pearl a thumbs up while still kissing his fiancé.

"When you want to hear about the house, join me inside." Pearl called out as she disappeared through the sliding door.

Olivia finally broke the kiss. "What is she talking about, Alex?"

He sighed. "This house is technically mine. And my house is Pearl's, kind of."

"I'm *kind of* lost, Alex." Olivia told him with a chuckle.

"In the inheritance, Pearl got to choose which house she wanted and she chose the yellow one, but I didn't feel I was ready for all of this space and the big yard yet so she agreed to stay here with Alice's help until I decided I was ready, with a wife, and maybe kids. And well, now I'm going to have a wife, so we need to make a decision."

Olivia walked back over to her chair and sat down, thinking for a minute. "Wow, I'm not sure. I mean, I love both houses, but do you think Pearl could stay here for another year or so?" she asked hopefully. "I just want it to be us together in the little yellow cottage for a while. And then we can maybe have kids and move to this house?"

Alex gave a sigh of relief. "That was exactly what I'd hoped you would say. Come on, let's go tell Pearl."

****

Olivia had to call her mother, not only to tell her about the engagement, but to see if she could arrange to get her inheritance early.

Charlotte picked up the phone after three rings. "Hello, darling how is Ketchikan?"

"Hi mama. It's great, I love it here."

"I'm so glad, Livia. You sound happier than I've heard you in years."

"I am, you'll never guess what happened."

"What dear? Tell me!" Charlotte demanded.

"Mama," she paused. "Alex asked me to marry him."

"And you said yes right?" her mother asked.

"Of course I did."

"Well good, I truly didn't see that coming, but I'm so happy for you both."

"Thanks mom, but I have a huge favor to ask now."

"Go on," Charlotte coaxed.

"What are the conditions under which I can get my inheritance a bit early?"

"Well, extreme financial need through no cause of your own, educational needs, buying a business in which you have an appropriate degree and two years' experience, an adoption or fertility treatment as long as you are over the age of twenty one, medical expenses and finally the executor can petition for release of any funds they deem necessary."

"And you are the executor?"

"Yes I am, why?"

"Well, I'm thinking of buying a diner here in town, but I don't know if it would still be available in November."

"That sounds like a good way to spend some of your money. And it meets the requirements, you've been working in restaurants since you were a teenager and you have a hospitality degree."

"That's what I was thinking," Olivia agreed.

"Could you send daddy and I all of the info you have on it so we could make sure it's a sound business?"

"Of course. I'll fax it to you as soon as I talk to the owner here in a bit."

"Does Alex know the owner?" Charlotte asked.

"Yeah, she is his Aunt Pearl's best friend."

"Oh okay, I trust Pearl's wisdom. I'll call her and talk to her about it too."

Olivia was getting the feeling that Pearl had also been a part of the set up. "So, you know Pearl, Mother?"

"Um, well, yes. We became fast friends over social media and on the phone."

"So she helped you get Alex and I back together? She was in on the plan this whole time?"

Charlotte let out a big sigh. "Yes dear, she was, as was Eleanor. I told Pearl who I was when I made the reservations and she agreed to help. We've talked three or four times a week since then."

Olivia laughed. "Well, I guess I should be grateful."

"Yes, you should dear."

Olivia couldn't believe her mother's gall but she didn't say anything more about it. "Okay mother, give Pearl a call, look over the stuff I fax to you and give me a call back with your decision."

"I'll call you in a couple of hours and we can see how things are going."

Olivia sat Alex down to finally tell him about the matchmaking scheme, but he already knew about Charlotte's role. Graham had told him on their flight to Seward. They agreed to have a talk with Pearl, but she somehow doubted they ever would. They were too happy and it was all water under the bridge.

****

Olivia and Alex decided a tour of the restaurant would be next on the agenda and Millie greeted them when they walked in the door.

"Millie, this is Olivia Mannon," Alex introduced.

"From the looks of it, she is the soon to be Olivia Paige," Millie said, smiling and pointing at the ring.

"True Millie, very true," Alex added.

"Well, it's nice to meet you dear!" Millie enthused, pulling Olivia into a hug.

The older woman immediately faxed all of the necessary information to Charlotte and then sat down and talked with the couple for a whole two hours. Right as they were about to leave, Charlotte called and gave the okay for Olivia to buy The Dock Stop, they would start the paperwork within a couple of days.

By the time all was said and done, they only had time for a quick tour of some of the non-tourist parts of town so Alex showed her some schools, the hospital and the major food and retail outlets and then they headed to Jason's house.

Olivia was welcomed warmly by Millie, Pearl, Jason's wife Marie, Mark's wife Alexa and three other women; Helen, the wife of the head of Ambulance Services at the local hospital, Susan, a teacher, and Lauren, a single mother of two who worked at The Dock Stop and rented a room from Millie.

They all pulled her into the living room and Alex disappeared into the garage with Jason, Mark and three other men.

"I just love when we get new people, it makes life a little more exciting around here," Alexa enthused.

"Where are you moving here from?" Helen asked.

"Just outside Vegas," Olivia answered.

"Wow, a lot of people are moving here from Nevada. Our new firefighter/paramedic supervisor will be moving here from the Vegas area. If I remember correctly he will be bringing a wife and a seven year old daughter. The wife is an ER nurse and we hope to get her on at the hospital."

"Olivia dear, what's wrong?" Pearl asked when she noticed her sitting there with her mouth open.

"Uh, Helen, do you know the name of the firefighter/paramedic" Olivia asked.

"I believe it was Graham Blake, Why?"

"Well shit!" Olivia exclaimed with a smile on her face.

"Do you know him dear?" Millie asked.

Olivia chuckled. "Yeah, I do, he's my brother-in-law. I had no idea they were moving here."

"He just accepted the position yesterday via a ship to shore call from somewhere near Seward," Helen told her.

Olivia was so excited, she and her big sister would be living in the same town. What a wonderful turn of events. "I think you guys are going to love Graham and Mari, they are really good people."

"Another person to add to the group, how fun!" Susan enthused.

The women continued to talk and get to know Olivia while the men grilled steaks and played basketball.

Dinner was a loud, rambunctious affair and when things wound down, Alex and Olivia decided it was time to call it a night and head back to the house. There were hugs and handshakes all around, and before they left Lauren pulled Olivia aside.

"You might hear some talk around the diner that I'm after Alex," she informed her future boss shyly. "I just want you to know that I was interested in him, but now that he has you, I'll back off. I want us to be friends, not enemies."

Olivia really liked Lauren, she was somehow innocent, experienced and scared all at the same time. She pulled the young girl into a hug.

"No worries, I hope we'll be great friends."

****

Alex pulled his truck into the driveway and turned it off. "I've been thinking," he turned to Olivia and grabbed her hand. "Would you be opposed to moving into the big house and letting Pearl live in the garage apartment. That way we could rent this house to Mari and Graham until they're ready to buy. The housing market here is a bit steep compared to Vegas and I know Graham has a house to sell first."

"What a great idea, Alex. Mari will probably want to buy once her inheritance isn't tied up anymore next year, but for now, that would be perfect." Olivia couldn't wait for her sister to get there. "Do you think Pearl would agree?"

"She already has. I talked to her right after you told me they were moving here, while you were talking to Lauren."

"Oh, I can't wait to talk to Graham and Mari about it."

"You won't have to wait long, they'll be here Wednesday and they booked a flight tour of Misty Fjord. They requested the owner and his beautiful assistant to accompany them."

Olivia shook her head. "She must be in love, she hates to fly."

Alex laughed. "But Pearl did warn them that it might be you and one of the other pilots. This is the time of year my regular client comes back."

"Regular client?" she asked.

"Yeah, a photographer from some nature magazine comes every year at this time and will only go out with me." He informed her. "I'm kind of hoping he will make it when you are gone to Nevada to wrap things up there because I'll be gone for four to six days."

"I think it sounds exciting!" Olivia enthused. "I wonder if I've ever seen his work."

"I'm sorry, I never asked him what publication he works for. I'll bring it up this time."

Olivia nodded then asked, "Why are we sitting here in the truck still?"

"Just wait a minute." And no sooner had he said it, than Olivia's Jeep pulled up, followed by another vehicle. Pearl got out of the Jeep and got into the other car with Mark and drove away. Olivia jumped out of the truck and ran over to her Jeep where she took the keys out of the ignition and put them in her pocket.

"All checked over and detailed for you." Alex said as he wrapped his arms around her. "How about we go inside now and celebrate our engagement?"

"I like that idea," she whispered.

They walked inside arm in arm and stood, kissing, in the foyer. Olivia pulled away when Alex's stomach growled. "I was so anxious to get you home, I didn't eat much at dinner. I think I'm going to make a ham sandwich, would you like one?"

"No, I'm okay," she answered sitting on the couch. "I'm just going to try to get a hold of Jackson and tell him about the engagement." She pulled out her phone and hit speed dial two. After twenty rings, she gave up. He was either in Anchorage or Denali and probably didn't have service. Finding Deborah and seeing his son was more important anyway.

"No luck huh?" Alex asked, sitting next to her on the couch.

"Nope, I'll try again tomorrow." She nestled up to his side while he ate his sandwich. "What a wonderful, but long, day."

"I think it'll get even better," he whispered in her ear. He couldn't wait to make love to her all over again. This times she would be his future wife.

"I'm sure it will be," she whispered back, while running her fingers up his thigh.

He inhaled sharply as they lightly brushed across his groin. With one hand she undid the snap and lowered his zipper, moving her fingers inside.

"Underwear today huh?" she asked, raising her eyebrow.

"To make it take longer to get to me," he joked. One of his hands held his sandwich and the other caressed her neck and ran down her chest where he started unbuttoning her shirt, exposing the purple lace bra underneath. "You look better in black. I think I'll have to take you out of this."

He smiled at her and started peeling her shirt off her shoulders, the last quarter of his sandwich now lay forgotten on the coffee table. "You see, this just won't do. It has to come off now." He pushed the straps down her arms and teased the top of her breasts, first with the tips of his fingers and then his lips. He worked his way up to her mouth, kissing her as he quickly unhooked the bra, peeling it off. He let out a low hissing breath. "Every time Doll, every last time I see you, I lose my breath."

Olivia shivered at his words and when he bent down to take a nipple into his mouth, she felt like she might never stop shaking.

"Right here, right now, or our bedroom," he asked as his lips moved down to her stomach.

"Right here, right now Alex, please."

This time he didn't have the patience to tease her. He only wanted to pleasure her.

Hours later as Olivia lay sleeping peacefully, Alex slipped out of bed and dressed.

"What's wrong, where are you going?" she mumbled as she saw him walking to the door.

"I just want some fresh air. Go back to sleep," he whispered.

She rolled over and fell asleep quickly, dreaming of a big wedding in their new backyard.

Chapter 13

Olivia reached out to touch Alex and found his spot cool and empty. Had he come back after getting fresh air? There were blackout curtains on the windows so she rolled over and looked at the clock on the night stand, it read nine a.m. He'd actually let her sleep in.

Her robe and slippers were on the chair in the corner so she grabbed them and slipped them on. In the hall, a light shone out of a room she hadn't explored yet. Olivia figured it must be Alex's office so she padded down there and peeked inside, but he wasn't there.

Masculine was the only word that could accurately describe the room; dark wood furniture, bookshelves lining the walls and a very large desk with a very large leather chair behind it. She couldn't help but walk over and drop into it. It was as comfortable as it looked. She twirled it around and checked out some of the books on the shelves behind her. Alex still had quite a collection, his small apartment in Henderson had been jam packed with books stuffed into every last nook and cranny.

She spun back around and planted her hands on the desk, the document laying there immediately caught her attention. A company named Foster's Aviation was looking to acquire property and five float planes. Her head spun and her mind went to dark places that it shouldn't have.

"Morning, Doll," Alex said from the doorway. "Did you sleep well?"

Olivia looked up from the desk with tears in her eyes. "You lied to me," she ground out.

"What are you talking about, Livia? I've never lied to you."

"You haven't changed at all," she yelled at him. "You're still a damn good for nothing slacker."

Alex looked like he'd been punched. She said the word that could change everything for them. "It seems you're the one who lied to me," he complained. "You really haven't changed a bit, you're still the same old bitch you always were."

Olivia flinched and then recovered, she had something on her mind that needed to be said. “Why Alex?” she cried. “You seemed to love what you do, you are good at it, and you *said* you loved it, why are you selling the business.”

“I’m not selling…you know what, forget it. I’m done. I can’t go through this again.” He was breathing hard when he walked out of the office, and a few minutes later she heard the front door slam.

She sat back down at the desk and cried. When the tears started to fall, she wasn’t sure if they would ever stop. She flashed through heartache, anger and back to heartache again. Why hadn’t he told her he was planning to sell the business? He completely led her to believe that he’d changed. Then it occurred to her that maybe he had only wanted revenge all this time. And now he had it! He used her, abused her and left her heartbroken just like she had done to him all those years ago. Did that mean they were even now?

Drying her tears she stood up and walked to the kitchen. As she poured herself a cup of coffee something caught her attention, a note in Alex’s handwriting was propped on the sugar bowl.

I'm leaving for a few days to let you make plans. Sorry things didn't work out.
Alex

She couldn't believe it was over and done with so quickly. A small part of her hoped they could talk after things cooled off, but that wasn't going to happen. Her big mouth had caused her trouble once again.

Her first task was to call her twin, talking to Jackson would help ease her mind, it always did. But when she couldn't reach him, she made the decision not to call her parents yet, and she decided that packing her bag was the only thing left to do. She would go home, lick her wounds and try to start over again.

When she was just about packed up she decided to call Pearl and say goodbye. She highly doubted the kind older woman could have been a part of any revenge plan. Paige Air Tours voicemail picked up after three rings. "Hey Pearl, it's Olivia, I don't know if you heard what happened, but I'm headed back to Nevada on the next available flight. I found out that Alex lied to me and planned to sell the business all along. I don't mind so much that he got rid of another job, but I can't believe he's giving up the happiness he seemed to have. Anyway, I said some awful things to him and he left to give me time to pack up and get out. I just wanted to say goodbye and thank you for your kindness. Oh, and Pearl, please tell Alex that I do still love him."

Olivia hung up the phone and put the last three things in her suitcase. She zipped it up and went to sit on the couch where she took the phone book from the end table and looked up airlines. The next available flight would leave in three hours so she booked it. She would have to leave the house soon though because she had to take a ferry to the airport. The Jeep would get her to the docks and then she would call Pearl so they could pick it up there later.

****

As soon as Pearl stepped foot in the office, she checked messages and when she heard what Olivia had to say, she collapsed into her chair. The young miss had it all wrong. Alex was selling the planes and all property that went with them, not the whole business, he would never do that. A whole new fleet was in the works, and why hadn't he set her straight and kept her from leaving. She had to get ahold of both of those stubborn fools and make them work it out. They would be miserable without each other.

As she was sitting there pondering her next move, the radio crackled and she heard Alex's voice come over the speaker. Day…engine…come in…and then it went dead. She thought for sure Alex would be at the big house licking his wounds, but that communication definitely came from him. She ran down to the dock and discovered The *Living Doll* was gone, so she ran back to the office and tried to reach Alex via radio and cellphone, both with no luck. He wasn't supposed to leave in one of the planes without leaving a plan at the office and a pin on the map with his destination. Damn him, how dare he risk his safety like that.

Pearl tried to call Olivia to see if she knew where he'd gone but was sent straight to voicemail and no one answered the house phone. Now what? She started to pace and think of people and places she could call. Mark and Jason were both out on tours so she tired a couple of Alex's other friends, none of which had heard from him. She was just about to panic when Jason walked in.

"Boy am I glad to see you, I received a jumbled distress call from Alex and I have no idea where he is. Did he by chance tell you where he went?"

"No, he didn't tell me, but I did see him at the Dock Stop with that photographer client Mr. Williams. I bet they went out for their annual trip."

"Damn him, he didn't tell anyone and didn't file a flight plan. What the hell was he thinking?" But she knew he hadn't been thinking at all because his heart was breaking.

"I think I know where they were planning to go this year, Pearl. I'm done for the day so I'll fly out there. It's about two hours away so just hang tight. I'll call or radio when I know more." Jason hurried out of the office, readied a plane and took off.

Pearl breathed a sigh of relief and sat down hard in her chair, calling the authorities to let them know who the jumbled distress call had come from. If it was a true mayday they would have heard it, but not necessarily known who or where it came from. At least something was being done now to make sure that Alex was okay, and that he and Olivia would to be able to talk things out again.

Pearl puttered around the office trying to finish up the days' work before Jason got back to her. She wanted to close up shop early, Mark could always turn his tickets in the next day if he had to.

The work was finished in record time and the minute she sat down to relax for a bit, the clock seemed to stop. She tried to get ahold of Alex again, but he still wouldn't answer. Apprehension started to creep into her mind because it wasn't like Alex to stray far from his plane while with this particular client. He didn't want to intrude on the man's artistic vision so he hung back at the campsite, it had always been that way.

The closer it got to the two hour mark, the more antsy Pearl got. Alex just had to be okay and he just had to get her message about Olivia. Then she could run right over to her and tell her that she'd misunderstood the whole thing. She knew Alex would regret letting her go, maybe not today or tomorrow, but sometime down the road, he would deeply regret it.

Pearl must have jumped a foot out of her chair when the radio crackled to life.

"Pearl, it's Jason. Pick up."

Pearl hurried over to the radio. "I'm here Jason, what's going on?"

"I found The *Living Doll*, seems they might have had engine trouble and the radio is completely dead. But Alex and Mr. Williams are nowhere to be found. I even flew around and didn't catch a glimpse of them." She heard him let out a loud sigh. "Pearl, there's an awful lot of blood here. Someone was hurt pretty badly. I'm really worried. We need to let the authorities know all of this and get a group together for a search. I'll be back in two hours to help organize. I've got a pilot friend in Juneau and he's going to do air searches in the meantime."

Pearl felt the tears starting, her boy could be bleeding to death as they spoke. She never had kids of her own, but she'd become a second mom to her nephew. "Oh God! He has to be okay Jason, he's all I have left!"

"I know Pearl. We'll get him home safe. Call the authorities and let them know for sure where the distress call came from and what I found, and everyone else you can think of. We'll meet at Alex's house in two hours."

"Okay Jason." She was shaking when she walked to her desk and called the authorities who would then filter it down through proper channels. Three calls later she had friends helping her spread the word through town. She would go to Olivia and ask her to help too.

When she arrived at the cottage, the Jeep was gone and she got a sinking feeling in the pit of her stomach. When she let herself in and searched the house, she found a note scribbled on the pad on the end table. Olivia had a flight out in an hour. Pearl had to hurry, the next ferry would be leaving for the airport in ten minutes. The whole way there she cursed herself for not programming Olivia's number into her phone, it was sitting on the desk at the office. The short ride across the channel was seemingly endless, but she finally made it.

****

Olivia was sitting just inside the airport trying to get up the courage to check in for her flight. How could she leave? Things couldn't be over just like that. But Alex had told her to go and after what she'd said to him, there was probably no way to fix things. She stood to gather her belongings to head up to the checkout counter.

Her heart was breaking to leave, but at least she had her family to go to. And then she remembered that Jackson wouldn't be home yet. He was the one she wished she could see the most.

"Olivia wait, you can't leave!"

She almost didn't turn around but Pearl had a certain desperation in her voice.

"I *have* to go Pearl," she stressed.

The look on the older woman's face said it all though. Something was very wrong.

"Alex is missing, and possibly injured!" Pearl exclaimed. "Please come back with me?"

Olivia's heart sank. "After what I said, he wouldn't want me there Pearl."

"Sweetie, it was all a huge misunderstanding. He isn't selling the business. I'll explain later, but right now we need to find him. Just come with me. Please?"

No matter how angry and hurt and confused she was, she couldn't leave while Alex was in danger. "Alright, let's go!"

Pearl filled Olivia in on what was going on during the ferry ride. Including the details about the sale of the planes. Olivia felt awful about what had happened. She had to at least apologize to Alex.

"So what do we do now? If one of them is bleeding severely, how long do they have before it's too late?" No matter how hard it was, she had to keep her panic pushed down. It wouldn't do anybody any good if she wasn't in her right mind.

"I really don't know sweetie," Pearl advised her. "The authorities are on it, Jason is on his way back to help organize local efforts, and a pilot friend is out looking for them right now. There really isn't much more we can do until we meet up with everyone else."

"You said he wasn't too far from Juneau right?" Olivia inquired.

"Yeah, what are you thinking," Pearl asked.

"John and Sue. They're close to Juneau, maybe they could do something to help. They love Alex."

"Great idea!" Pearl pulled out her phone. "Damn I don't have them in my new phone. Do you have their number?

"No, Alex has it by the house phone though," she told Pearl. "I'll call them as soon as we get back."

Olivia's head was spinning. The man she loved was lost in the wilderness and possibly bleeding profusely, if not, his client was, and she had been thinking of leaving him. Hell, she'd called him the one name that was unforgiveable. Why did she do that? Why didn't she just calmly ask him to explain things? "Oh God!"

"What's wrong?" Pearl asked taking Olivia's shaking hand in her own.

"I almost made the biggest mistake of my life didn't I? I can't believe I overreacted so much."

Pearl hugged her and patted her shoulder. "It's okay sweetie."

"I told him he was a good for nothing slacker. Why did I say that, why did I act like that. I might not trust in people, but I don't usually fly off the handle."

"You were scared." Pearl stated. "You took the first opportunity to protect your heart, even if you weren't completely aware of it."

"You mean I found the first reason I could to call things off because I was afraid of getting hurt still?" she asked.

"Exactly."

Olivia knew the older woman was right. As much as she loved Alex and Ketchikan, her life had been unexpectedly changed in a short amount of time. She was so used to being disappointed and hurt that she didn't wait for it to happen again, she just created a situation that allowed her to leave. She was being a coward.

It wasn't like her to run from things, or was it? When she really thought about it, she'd been running from personal demons for a long time and she had to put a stop to that right now. She loved Alex and couldn't let her old life interfere with her new one anymore, if he agreed to take her back after all she'd said, that is.

Pearl and Olivia agreed to meet at Alex's house after leaving the ferry and when they arrived, one right after the other, there were already fifteen other cars parked along the street, their drivers waiting to be let into the house to make plans to find Alex and his photographer client.

The first thing Olivia did was call John and Sue, only to get no answer at their airfield, the result was the same when she tried their home. Desperation started to overtake her until Pearl wrapped her in a warm hug.

"What if we're too late?" Olivia whispered.

"Not going to happen," Pearl whispered back. She had to believe that.

Millie kept busy making food and drinks for the people coming and going while Pearl, Jason and Olivia made plans. Some friends where headed out in helicopters, some in boats and others in planes to look for the two missing men. A few were manning phones and the rest flew out to be dropped off to search on foot. There was a sense of camaraderie overlaying the sense of desperation to bring them both home alive.

About three hours after Olivia and Pearl arrived back at the cottage, they received news that a backpack and water logged cell phone were found. The backpack was believed to be the photographer's carrying his equipment and the phone was Alex's. They were found along a river about a quarter of the way between where The *Doll* was found and John and Sue's. They all prayed that Alex was headed there to try and get help from his friends.

Everyone hoped news would continue to trickle in, but it didn't. Olivia was getting frustrated and tired and every time another hour passed, her frustration grew. She hadn't been able to eat more than a bite or two all day which didn't help matters any. How come they weren't finding them? They couldn't have gotten too far from where they found the backpack and phone, one of them was injured after all. And had the authorities even tried to get ahold of John and Sue? The tempo her mind was keeping was starting to drive her insane. She paced inside, outside and everywhere in between, trying to keep the tears at bay. They just had to find him, it was almost midnight and it was cold outside. Her heart ached thinking of the two men suffering in any way.

"Olivia dear, they think they are getting closer, they found a bloody bandage caught on a tree branch and it looked like the bleeding had slowed greatly from the original scene." She turned Livia to face her. "Why don't you get some sleep? Being tired and overwrought isn't going to help anyone."

"I can't sleep Pearl, not until I know he's okay. I keep thinking that I might not get the chance to apologize, the chance to show him that I still love him"

"At least go lay down sweetie. You need to rest and wearing a path in the floorboards has got to be exhausting."

Olivia knew Pearl was right. She really should at least lay down for a while. If she got too restless she could always get up and pace again. "Okay Pearl, but if you hear anything, come get me, you have to promise me!"

"I promise," Pearl assured. "Now go."

Olivia walked back into the house and went into the master bath to wash her face and then she kicked her shoes off and lay down on her bed, Alex's bed. He would probably never want her in it again. The tears she felt threatening never came, but the sleep came quick and hard. She never felt it when at two in the morning Pearl came in to shake her awake.

"How did she take it?" Millie asked when Pearl came back to the living room.

"I couldn't wake her, she must have been exhausted. I'll just let her sleep, she'll find out soon enough."

"Okay, sounds like a good plan," Millie stated. "I'm going to get on out of here, if you need anything just call."

"I will my friend. I will."

Chapter 14

Olivia lay sleeping in Alex's bed. Her hands were curled under her cheek and although she was sound asleep her mind was still working, hoping that Alex would be okay.

"Doll, wake up."

"Alex?"

"Hi Doll."

"You're back!" She squealed.

"I came to tell you that I'm sorry for everything that happened earlier. I still love you Olivia and I always will. You're my *Living* Doll."

"Alex, why can I barely see you? You look like you're fading."

"I have to go now, Olivia. Just remember I'll always love you."

"Alex, what's going on? Please tell me."

"I have to go now, Doll, I didn't make it. I'll be with you always though. I love yo..."

"No!" The piercing scream permeated the air in the quiet Ketchikan neighborhood. Pearl, sleeping on Alex's couch, swore she felt the windows rattle. "Come back, Alex!" she screamed over and over.

"Doll, wake up! Doll! It's okay. I'm right here." Exhaustion had claimed Alex as soon as he laid down next to Olivia and he'd gathered her into his arms and slept until her screams woke him.

"Alex?" She reached out and touched him; his face, his chest, and his arms. "You're really here, you aren't leaving me."

"Of course not, Livia. I love you so much."

"But you came to me, you were, you were dead. You didn't make it." The tears were flowing and her voice came out in broken sobs.

"It was just a dream sweetheart. Mr. Williams was injured, not me. I'm just exhausted from having to get him out of there, but I'll be good as new in a few hours."

Olivia dropped her head to his chest and cried. "I'm so sorry Alex, I have so much I need to say to you."

"It can wait Love, let's just sleep some more and then we can have brunch and talk."

"Okay," she choked out and snuggled deeper into Alex's side. They both fell asleep and Olivia didn't wake again until ten a.m.

****

"Love, it's time to get up. We don't want to sleep the day away."

Olivia stretched and smiled. The dream she'd had of Alex dying still weighed heavy on her mind, but she was so happy that he was still there and that he still loved her.

"Good morning. Are you feeling better?"

"Yep! Fully recharged, I just needed some sleep."

"I'm starving." She claimed as she rose from the bed. "I think a shower is in order then I want to get something to eat."

"Brunch is ready, so how about we eat and then you can take a shower," he suggested coming up to her and giving her a kiss.

"That depends, what's for brunch?"

"Chocolate chip pancakes, hash browns, and my famous veggie mix scrambled eggs."

"Hmm, I think the shower is going to have to wait. I can't resist your veggie mix eggs or your chocolate chip pancakes." She kissed him, grabbed his hand and dragged him to the dining room. Sitting on the table, next to her plate was a single pink rose.

"Oh Alex,"

"When I called the house to tell everyone I was on my way home, Pearl said you were here and that you were sad. All of the flower shops were closed that late so when I woke up this morning, I ran to grab one before I cooked breakfast."

"Thank you, Alex." She picked it up and brought it to her nose. "Absolutely beautiful."

"I'm glad you like it," he whispered.

As they settled in to breakfast Olivia decided she wanted to hear what had happened to him, before they talked about the state of their relationship. "Tell me what happened yesterday."

"Well, I met up with Mr. Williams at The Dock Stop and we decided to head on out instead of waiting until today like he'd originally planned. The *Living Doll* started to have problems so I landed about a mile from where we should have ended up. We figured it was close enough and I would try to fix her or call for help when the trip was over."

"Jason said the engine's gone and the radio was broken." Olivia told him.

"Yeah, I found that out much later, after the accident. Anyway, I set up camp and he started taking pictures." Alex paused and took a deep breath. "He came back to get his tripod and when he was setting it up, it snapped in half. A jagged edge caught his arm and tore him from the wrist to the inside of the elbow."

"Oh my God. The poor man must have been scared to death."

"He was. We weren't sure what kind of damage it could have done, especially at the wrist, and it was bleeding so much he started to get faint almost immediately. I bound the wound to try to slow the bleeding but he was so weak. I had to create a makeshift gurney out of a tent and we started the trek to John and Sue's. It's a good thing I knew that area or I'm not sure what would have happened."

"So Mr. Williams is okay?" Olivia asked.

"Yeah, he received some blood and a lot of stitches. He should be good as new in a few weeks."

"I'm just so glad you're both safe and sound. I don't know what I would have done if I lost you."

Alex reached across the table and took her hand in his. "Being out there, not knowing what would happen to Mr. Williams, not knowing if we would be able to make it over the river, I had a lot of time to think. I realized that for some reason, whether you are a materialistic snob or a kind, gentle soul, I love you. All of those things make up who you are and I love every bit of you."

Olivia smiled. "I'm not even offended that you called me a snob, because truthfully, I used to be. And I was yesterday too. I was scared Alex, and I didn't even realize it. I found the first possible reason to run and I took it." She squeezed his hand. "I've spent most of my life feeling guilty and being afraid and that affected how I lived my life. I truly am changing Alex, but I need you to be patient, it isn't going to be an overnight transformation."

"I know Doll, and I forgot that briefly yesterday. I should have just stayed and explained things to you, but I had this flashback to when we were together the first time and it threw me off." He pulled her hand to his lips and kissed it. "My biggest fear is that this is all a dream, that we never met again and we never got our second chance. Yesterday, for the briefest of seconds, that fear started to come true and it scared me. I'm sorry, Livia."

"I guess neither of us is quite as over our past as we thought. But I think this whole episode helped and now we know what to watch out for. We're going to be just fine Alex!"

"Yes we are. I can't wait until you become my wife, if you still want to marry me, that is."

"Of course I still want to marry you, nothing has changed there. We just need to remember that we have to work hard to put the past in the past and forge a new future for ourselves."

"Exactly. Now I have a favor to ask."

"Okay," she hedged.

"Will you help me pick out The *Living Doll Two*?" he asked.

"Of course? Was she that badly damaged?" Olivia inquired.

"As much as I hate to admit it, she's just getting old and I don't want to keep up with her anymore. We have a second chance at our relationship so I think having The *Living Doll Two* is fitting somehow."

Olivia smiled. "You know, I think you're right."

They cleaned up after brunch together and then went to Alex's office to look online at the planes Alex wanted to buy. After an hour of talking, figuring and searching, Olivia chose the next *Living Doll* floatplane. She was beautiful and they couldn't wait to get her and take her up. It would be awhile though because it would take time to finalize the deal.

Alex was acting sad and she wondered if it was about losing the original Living Doll.

"What's wrong, Alex?"

"After everything that happened, I started to miss my parents. Would you come with me to the cemetery, I'd kind of like to see them."

"Sure, I'd love to pay my respects."

Olivia drove them in her Jeep, to a flower shop and then to the cemetery. She dropped Alex off close to where his parents were buried and went to park the car. She wanted to hang back and give him time to visit them alone.

****

Alex walked over to a row of three graves. They all had the last name Paige, engraved on them. His mother, his father and his uncle. He could easily have been the next one if they hadn't made it out of the wilderness safely. Mr. Williams wasn't the only one in danger, the elements could have killed Alex just as easily as a wound could have.

"Hey mom, dad, Uncle Peter, I really needed to see you. A client and I had a close call and it made me think about you guys, I really miss you." He smiled, even though he felt so incredibly sad. "There is so much I want to be able to tell you, I wish I could do it face to face," he whispered as he sat down, facing all three graves, and putting a flower on each. "Olivia came back to me guys. But then you knew she would didn't you? You always said we were meant to be. Hell, you were probably working with Charlotte and Pearl to make it happen weren't you?"

He heard footsteps and turned to see Olivia walking up the incline. She stopped and he motioned her forward. When she reached the row of headstones, she sat next to Alex and he put his arm around her. "We're getting married mom." A single tear slipped down his face and he turned to Olivia. "My mom made me promise that if I ever got married, I had to tell her beforehand. I promised I'd never elope." He chuckled. "When I went to college in Vegas, I think she was worried that I would head to a quickie chapel with the first girl I saw."

Olivia chuckled too, and put her flowers on the three graves. "Cindy and Alex, I just want to thank you for giving your son to the world. He is my everything, I don't know what my life would be like without him." She reached over and wiped the tears from under his eyes. "I think they're happy that we're back together. I can feel it."

"I know they are," Alex agreed. He stood and pulled her to stand by his side. "We should probably be headed back. Would you like to come to Juneau with me to say thanks to John and Sue? I thought maybe we could have dinner with Mari and Graham while they're there."

"Yes! That would be perfect, I can't wait to see my sister again."

Within the hour they were in one of the spare Paige Air Tours planes, headed to Juneau.

****

John and Sue met the couple at the docks and Olivia rushed to hug them. "Thank you so much for finding Alex. How did you even know he was missing?"

"The pilot that was out looking for him while Jason headed back to Ketchikan, is our son."

"Well, thank him for me too then!"

"Will do." John assured. "So what do you guys have planned for today?"

Olivia smiled. "My sister and her new husband are in town and we thought we would have dinner with them."

"Well then that gives you plenty of time to come with us in the new helicopter to the Juneau Icefield."

"You got it!" Alex exclaimed. "The new one's here?"

"Yep, arrived this morning. Want to take it for a spin?"

Alex looked at Olivia and smiled. "I think I'll just enjoy the sights with my finance this time. I would love to take it up some other time though."

Sue grabbed Olivia's left hand and gave Alex a dirty look. "Your grandma's ring, very nice boy, I just think I should have known sooner than this young man!"

Alex smiled meekly. "Yeah, sorry, I had other things on my mind yesterday."

"Well then you're forgiven." Sue smiled at him as she hugged Olivia. "As long as I'm invited to the wedding."

"Of course you are," Alex stressed. "Now let's go, Olivia has never seen the icefield before."

John expertly guided them up in the helicopter and pointed out all of the important sites during the thirty five minute flight to their destination.

"Have you ever been on this tour before, Alex?"

"Yeah, John used to take us all the time when I was younger. I never get tired of it."

"I can see why," Olivia enthused. "I don't think I would ever get tired of it either."

Alex squeezed her hand. "Any time you want to see it, just say the word."

John landed the helicopter on a glacier and Olivia felt the peace seeping inside.

"Can we just stay here, Alex?"

He chuckled. "Probably not a good idea Doll. But in a few minutes we can get out of the helicopter and explore a bit if you'd like."

Olivia had one of the best times of her life exploring the river of ice as the glacier was called. It was truly a trip she would never forget. And by the end of it she felt as if she finally knew John and Sue well, they were her family now too.

"Can we drop you off somewhere," John asked as they arrived back at the airfield.

"Yeah, we're going to meet Mari and Graham at Peterson's, if it's not too much trouble."

"Nah, not at all son. Sue and I are going out for a romantic dinner for two at Gino's, so we'll drop you off on the way."

Olivia watched the older couple nuzzle and kiss each other. "I hope we're like that in twenty-five years," she whispered to Alex.

"I'm sure we will be. I don't think I will ever be able to keep my hands off of you."

****

Olivia sat at their table, her eyes never leaving the door. She could not wait to see her sister. They'd only been apart for a few days, but so much had happened.

Mari walked through the door first, followed quickly by Graham. Olivia stood and waited for her sister to reach the table, and when she did they hugged for a long moment before sitting down.

"It's so good to see you." Olivia enthused. "How is the honeymoon going?"

"The honeymoon is great! Having no drama and no mothers on the cruise is making it a wonderful experience this time around."

Olivia laughed. "Yeah, I must admit that having mother thousands of miles away is kind of refreshing."

While the sisters talked about the engagement and Mari and Graham's move to Ketchikan, the men caught up on old times. They were poker buddies at one point and hadn't talked much since Alex left town.

"So do you have a wedding date yet?" Mari asked.

"No," Olivia admitted. "But I was thinking maybe in September after you guys arrive and get settled in. If that's not too soon," she said, looking at Alex.

"I think September would be prefect," Alex agreed. "I was thinking maybe the tenth, which was my dad's birthday."

"The tenth it is!" Olivia confirmed.

"Now all we have to do is find a place to live," Mari bemoaned. "I hate house hunting and we have to hope the house sells before we leave, it's just going to turn into one big mess."

"We have a house you can use until you find one of your own, no pressure and no hurry," Alex informed them. "It's a four bedroom, two bath cottage in a great neighborhood. We live there now, but will be moving to the new house in the next couple of weeks."

"Really," Graham asked? "That would be great. I want to take our time before we make that kind of investment."

"Absolutely. It's yours if you want it. You can explore it when you're in Ketchikan on Wednesday."

Alex and Olivia told the couple more about the cottage and before anyone wanted to admit it, the time to get back on the ship drew near. Alex and Graham shook hands while Mari and Olivia hugged each other goodbye, until they would meet up again on Wednesday. When they walked out of the restaurant the wind and rain hit them hard.

“Great, I don’t think we should fly home in this Doll, we might want to stay the night.”

“I know just the place!”

“We could always stay with John and Sue.”

“No way, let them be alone tonight. You know, I always used to say that I was a suite at a five star resort and you were camp outdoors. Tonight you’ll be staying on my turf.”

“Doll, Juneau doesn’t have any five star resorts.”

“There’s an inn that’s close enough. If it was rated, it would be a five star. And I just happen to know they have a room open. Wait here and I’ll set it up.”

“This ought to be good.” Alex lamented.

Ten minutes later, they caught a cab to a beautiful seaside inn where everything was devoted to luxury, from the high thread count sheets to the complimentary champagne and caviar.

“So how did you manage to get the room?” Alex asked, amazed that she’d actually pulled it off.

"The couple next to us at dinner had reservations but didn't want to pay that much for it so they considered cancelling, but didn't want to get charged. I overheard their dilemma and offered to take it off their hands. Worked out well for all of us."

Alex chuckled. "You always did have super hearing, and other super abilities. Think you can show me some of those tonight? You know, between the expensive sheets?"

Olivia just chuckled and pointed out the window to the Inn. "It's so beautiful."

"And so are you." Alex whispered before they stepped out of the taxi.

****

"This place is amazing!" Alex admitted reluctantly.

"I had fun camping and you will have fun here. I guarantee it," Olivia assured him.

"I'm intrigued," he said softly as he wrapped his arms around her. "If I have my way, I'm not sure how much luxury suite we'll see though." He turned her in his arms and kissed her, slowly peeling off her clothes, piece by piece.

"I'm going to take a shower, will you join me?" she asked.

"No, I think I'll stay out here. I don't think I could be in there with you and not do something."

"We can do whatever you want in there, it's your night." She said softly.

Alex groaned and started to undress himself. "Are you sure?"

"I am, I'll meet you in there."

Alex walked into the bathroom a bit hesitantly. Olivia didn't like this, they'd only had shower sex a hand full of times. He didn't want to make her uncomfortable. It looked like compromise truly was going to be the key to their relationship.

"Get in here Alex, I want you," she called out.

He slid the shower door open and stepped in, barely having time to slide it closed before Olivia was on him, kissing and teasing him with her hands. He grabbed her waist to steady her and went to work on her body with his mouth. While he teased her breasts she stroked him until he ached to have all of her. He pressed her back against the wall and pinned her hands above her head. With one swift movement he was buried deep within her. "Yes," he hissed and thrust swiftly again and again. His lips seared a path across her jaw and bit gently at the pulse point. The warm water cascaded over both of them and a moan escaped her lips. She wanted to touch him to caress his working muscles, but he had her hands pinned. She truly didn't mind at all, he was taking care of her every need and driving her mad in the process.

"Alex, I need more, please."

He slowed his pace, teasing her. His teeth nipped at her breasts and he bit down firmly, but gently on her nipple.

"Yes, Oh God! Alex please!"

He thrust harder until until he thought he might go mad, and then his grip on her hands relaxed. When she came with a sigh, and a shudder that shook her from head to toe, he caught her by the waist and came with her, into their new world.

They were finally completely in sync in every way. Not just physically, but emotionally. They were once worlds apart, but now, finally, they were two people who had forged a new world full of peace, to live in together. Forever.

Epilogue

Charlotte Mannon's Journal

August 20, 2011 – I talked to Olivia late tonight. The grand re-opening of her restaurant, The Dock Stop went perfectly. I wish we could have been there to celebrate with her but since it seems we will be headed to Ketchikan for a wedding soon, we decided to just wait.

September 10, 2011 – What a wonderful, exhausting day. At ten a. m. Alaskan Time, Olivia and Alex exchanged vows. Olivia's dress was simple, yet beautiful, made of white silk and Alex looked so handsome in his white tuxedo. The best thing though, was that all of the Mannon's and Blake's were able to be there and I finally got to meet Pearl in person. She, Eleanor and I get along fabulously. On second thought, I think the best thing was that Olivia agreed to go camping for the honeymoon!!!

October 1, 2011 – I called Alex and Olivia to congratulate them. They now have a fleet of six new babies – five floatplanes and one helicopter. As for real babies, Olivia says we'll have to wait a year before they even try to give us a grandchild. We'll see about that.

April 3, 2012 – I'm in Ketchikan for the birth of Mari's twins and Olivia just found out that she is pregnant! It looks like I will be a grandma again in January 2013. I'm just wondering if she'll have twins or not. Woo Hoo! I'm loving being a grandma.

About the Author

JJ Ellis is first and foremost the mother to five children, four girls and one boy. She is also a wife, blogger and now author. *Alaskan Ambush,* her second novel, is the second in the series about the Mannon children and their matchmaking mother. Stay tuned for the third book in the series *Stormy Seas,* featuring Abigail and Sam.

JJ lives with her husband, kids and one crazy mutt in Casper, WY. She enjoys reading, writing, computing and graphic design. She is the author of a blog entitled *Adventures of a Broken Housewife.*

You can contact her at:
http://www.brokenhousewife.com
http://www.writerjjellis.com
brokenwifeandmom@gmail.com

3091236R00177

Made in the USA
San Bernardino, CA
04 July 2013